ICE
GUARDIAN SECURITY DEFENDERS
BOOK ELEVEN

KRIS MICHAELS

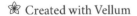 Created with Vellum

CHAPTER 1

Concealed in the shadows, Ice stifled a yawn as he listened to his target bang the hell out of a woman in his room. He nonchalantly tossed his blade into the air, watching the path of its finely balanced steel, and deftly caught it while his target enjoyed his nightly routine. After the man was done, the guards would escort the woman out, close and lock the doors behind them, and stand guard outside that wing of the house.

When the crescendo of grunts and pitiful cries finally reached an apex and the sounds of rutting stopped, Ice rose from the couch where he'd been lounging. Silently, he moved, positioning himself in a corner of the room the guards couldn't see when they entered.

Straining a bit, he heard the man speak in rapid Russian. He glanced at his watch and started timing. Forty-three seconds later, his target's study door opened. He listened as the guards moved to the bedroom door and knocked. The door opened and closed. The woman they escorted out of the bedroom was crying softly. He waited until the guards closed the doors and the lock engaged before moving.

Ice went to the bedroom door and opened it. After slipping inside, he made his way to the bathroom. The shower was running, and the balding, potbellied, married senior adviser to the president of Russia was sitting on the toilet. His feet were visible just beyond the half wall built for privacy.

Moving silently, Ice dropped down and crossed the room. He crouched behind the partial wall beside the toilet, took his blade, and lifted it, looming over the half wall. His target startled, but only after Ice grabbed what hair was left on that head, yanked it back, and sliced his throat. He was used to the sounds the knife made. The resistance and the force needed to kill, not maim, made a sluicing sound, along with the snapping of cartilage and the rasp of flesh against the blade. The escape of blood was instantaneous. The gurgling sound of air leaving the man's windpipe and the distinct coppery scent of blood registered, but no other sounds could be heard over the shower.

Ice held the man's head back until his pupils became fixed and lifeless. Then, he dropped his hold, and his target slumped forward and rolled off the toilet into an ever-widening pool of his own blood. Ice casually walked around the growing puddle. He rinsed off his knife in the shower's warm water, then turned off the spray. Using one of the man's pristine white towels, he wiped off his knife and gloves.

As he stared at the man on the floor, Ice felt nothing. He had no remorse, no excitement, nothing other than a slight sense of satisfaction about completing his assignment. Taking a life had never been a problem for him. He killed on principle. If the Council targeted someone and he was told to take them out by his handlers at Guardian —he did. People like that bastard who used their positions to commit horrendous atrocities against the human race deserved the sentences they received.

Ice walked through the bedroom to the study, where he exited through the window he'd entered. Balanced on a four-inch ledge outside the third story, traversing the outside of the building was more dangerous than completing his mission. He moved slowly, ensuring his toe and finger holds were secure before moving from one window to another. Three sets of glass panes farther along the small ledge, he paused. The politician's wife was busy in bed with someone else. Ice would have rolled his eyes, but he'd save it for when he was on the ground. Losing his balance would be an abrupt end to his career.

He moved from ledge to ledge. His fingers ached, and his toes—wrapped in specially-made bendable, gripping-soled boots—were ready to be off the damn building. Rounding the corner, he grabbed the old-fashioned bronze drainpipe and carefully lowered himself to the ground. Crouched where he dropped, he worked his fingers as he watched for any guard who might have finally decided to do his job and patrol the area. There was none. It was too cold and too late to worry about anyone in Moscow daring to enter the premises.

Ice pulled his black ski cap down over his face. There were two cameras on the other side of the fence. If he dropped down in the wrong place or had to change locations going over the nine-foot brick wall, he could be caught on film.

Examining the side yard one more time and satisfied he was alone, he stood, rocked back and forth, and then sprinted to the wall. His foot hit the wall about four feet up, and he lunged for the top. Gripping one of the finial-tipped bars at the top of the wall, he pulled himself to the crest. The wide bottom and draping branches of a fir tree blocked any visual of him dropping to the ground.

Ice stayed behind the tree for thirty minutes, watching and waiting. The target wouldn't be found until morning. He had plenty of time to make sure he left without a trace. When he was convinced it was safe to move, he took off his hat, reversed his coat, now brown instead of black, and bloused his jeans at the top of his climbing boots. Ice slid with his back to the tall brick fence, out from behind the fir tree. He took three steps to the corner of the block, a turn to the right, and vanished.

Walking for over two hours—and avoiding the precariously few cameras in the city—wasn't diffi-cult. Ice finally arrived at his "borrowed" and ancient Lada Granta. The small car was burgundy once upon a time. The passenger side mirror and the front bumper were missing, but it ran when he hotwired it, so it had become his transportation for the evening. The trip back to where he'd liberated the Granta was quick. Ice left a small bundle of rubles tucked in the well-used ashtray and walked away.

He pulled his cell phone out of his pocket and powered it up once he'd disappeared into the Russian forest near where he'd returned the car.

A vibration hit his hand as soon as the device was on, which was more than unusual. He glanced down at the text.

>>> THE ROSE. ASAP.

WELL, shit. Ice sighed. He'd been summoned. If he were supposed to call, they'd have said contact. Just stating the location gave him his marching orders. He glanced at the date and time it had been sent. Two weeks ago. He keyed in his text to Anubis.

>> MISSION COMPLETE. En route.

. . .

HE TURNED off the phone and rolled his shoulders. *Why the hell did he need to go to the Rose?* Ice trudged through the forest, abandoning his gloves and hat in the darkness. He opened his vehicle, reached into the glove box, and grabbed the apple he'd put in there before driving out. Ice chomped on the fruit as he pulled out of the small enclave of trees he'd parked within. He had hours to go before he'd be able to board a plane. The apple wouldn't be enough, and Russian cuisine was at the top of the list of things he disliked eating. A lot of nothing followed Russian food on his do-not-eat list. Maybe he'd only had bad food while in Russia, but he was pretty positive he'd found the one kind of food he didn't like.

Ice leaned back as he drove. The road was empty, and he had papers that made him legitimate. He had no worries, and he'd been looking forward to crossing the border, eating decent food, relaxing for a while, and then maybe heading to France or Spain before returning to the States. French food was rich, layered in flavor, and delicious—a personal favorite. Spanish cuisine had an earthy essence and warm spice—particularly the

Basque Country on the border of France and Spain. The seafood and meat dishes were incredible, but it was bliss paired with Txakoli, a sharp white wine. Ice bit into the apple. The night had just turned into a royal pain in his ass.

ICE DISLIKED this portion of the journey to the Rose. The driver was, as always, Thanatos, yet they didn't talk. Ice was ensconced in the back of a blacked-out SUV. He had no idea where in the desert they were going. That shook him the first time he'd attended training at the Rose. Subsequent travels were less stressful but equally uncomfortable. A hazard of the profession—he needed to know what was happening around him at all times. This leg of the journey didn't help. It also didn't help that the travel time varied by hours each time he was taken to the Rose. There was no way he'd be able to pinpoint where the facility was even if he wanted to do so. He understood the precautions, especially after the Siege. But it sucked donkey balls not to know where he was going.

When the vehicle finally slowed to a stop and

the engine cut off, Ice was more than ready to get out of the damn thing. The intensely bright Arizona, New Mexico, or whatever fucking state they were in sun nearly blinded him.

"Fury and Anubis are waiting for you below," Thanatos said before turning and walking away.

"Great seeing you again, too." Ice threw the sarcastic comment to the assassin's back.

Thanatos raised a hand in acknowledgment and headed in the opposite direction of where Ice needed to go. Ice headed for the only access point to the lower facility. He was positive there were other entry and exit points, but he'd never needed to know where they were, so he was never told. He liked that. He didn't want to know the fluff. Just give him the minimum he needed to do his job. In fact, he'd rather not talk to anyone. He had exactly seven friends and worked damn hard to trust their partners or spouses. Mostly, he'd succeeded, although he wasn't comfortable around the ones who didn't work in his profession.

He waved at the doctor in the office. Fury's wife, if the rumor was to be believed. The redhead received a very wide berth from everyone at the facility, so he had no doubt it was true. He wouldn't test the old man. No one in their right mind would.

The descent was quick and substantially cooler. When the door opened, he saw Anubis waiting for him.

"What's the scoop?" Ice asked as he exited the elevator. He didn't like being recalled. Something was fucking up.

"Fury will brief you." Anubis led the way to a secure area, which was redundant in one of the most secure locations in the world, but whatever.

The door opened and closed behind them. He heard the lock and waited for the light to turn green. When it did, the door on the other side of the passageway opened, revealing Fury, who nodded to a seat at the conference table as Anubis took his seat on Fury's right.

"Care to tell me why I've been called to the principal's office?" Ice dropped into the seat.

Fury tossed him a package of cookies. "Stop being a bitch."

Ice opened the cellophane and grabbed a chocolate and vanilla cream double-stuffed wonder out of the plastic tray. "Okay, you're almost forgiven."

"You and Asp could eat your way through this

facility's emergency stores in a week." Anubis chuckled as he leaned back.

"That so?" Ice hadn't met Asp. Smoke, Thanatos, Anubis, and Fury were his only connection to the ancient ones.

"The reason you were brought out here was to detail an assignment." Fury pushed a button, and a screen woke up under the table where his cookies were sitting. Ice took another one and moved the package. "Do you know what the Five Eyes are?"

"Reading, writing, and arithmetic?" Ice said before popping another cookie into his mouth. Fury lifted his gaze and leveled a pissed-off look at Ice. A smile spread across Ice's face. He wasn't intimidated. "I take that look to mean no."

Fury drew a deep breath and closed his eyes. Ice could see the man mentally counting to twenty. His brain was sending up smoke signals. He'd chill for a while, maybe.

"No." Fury leaned back in his chair. "The Five Eyes originally was a group consisting of the United States, the United Kingdom, Canada, Australia, and New Zealand. The intent of the group was to disseminate signal technology. Intercepting coded messages and the like during World War Two's aftermath and the Cold War. It still exists to this day, with more members. Successful for the most part in disseminating and sharing critical information keeping the allies informed on matters of international interest."

Ice put the cookies down as his eyes zeroed in on a small refrigerator. He got up and went over to it, speaking as he walked. "Score one for the good guys." What else was he supposed to say? He grabbed two waters from the fridge and returned to his seat. He downed the first bottle in one go. "Why are you telling me this?"

"Because that organization has detected an anomaly. Each time this anomaly, or whatever it is, activates, consequences happen."

"Consequences, as in?" Ice grabbed another cookie.

"An entire village was wiped out in Africa." Fury brought up slides depicting the crime. "A cartel struck a village in Mexico. There were no survivors and no news coverage. Then, there was a volatile collapse of a government in South America. A town in Siberia wiped out."

"So, money or communications are being transmitted. To who and from who?" Ice asked before popping another cookie into his mouth.

"Why haven't the computer geeks been able to crack this code?"

"Because the code no longer exists." Fury's response made no sense.

"Then, how are you going to track this person or entity?"

"That's why you're here."

Ice stopped chewing and turned to look at Fury. "Say what, now?"

"You will work with Flack and Smith to track down this entity and take them out. The Council has coded them."

"But you don't know who it is or how big it is." Ice frowned.

"Correct. It will take patience."

"Patience isn't my forte. Flack can track this." Ice shrugged his shoulders. "He has Smith to do the leg work. I'm not an investigator; I'm a terminator."

"This time, you're both. Flack isn't in the field, and Smith can't work there. He's too recognizable. You're tapped for this assignment. Deal with it."

Ice put his cookies down and drank his water as a string of ten thousand curse words flew through his mind. "I'm not suited for this mission."

"You will do what you are told," Fury countered. Ice locked glares with Fury, and neither of them blinked.

Anubis finally sighed. "You two can do the death stare on each other all you like. The fact remains that you, Ice, have been given this mission."

Ice turned his head and looked at Anubis. "I don't have patience."

"Then you better learn it," Fury hissed.

Ice whipped around and hissed back, "Did you?"

Fury's lip curled up. "Yeah, and it sucks. Swallow the pill and do as you've been told."

Ice narrowed his eyes and growled, "Fine. I'll do it. But I won't like it."

"Nobody asked you to like it." Fury hit a button, and the door opened. Obviously, that was his dismissal. Well, good, because he'd probably say something that would get him killed. Not that he wouldn't go down without a fight, but the ancient assassin was legendary and still looked like he was in peak physical condition.

Ice grabbed his cookies and walked out the door. He waited for the door to close and the one that led into the Annex to open. Exiting, he turned right, heading toward the bunkrooms. He'd claim one, get some real food, and hit the hay since his return flight wasn't until tomorrow. Somehow, he'd figure out the assignment. At least he got to kill the bastard or bastards causing his current headache. So, there was something to look forward to.

* * *

FURY WATCHED the door close behind the young assassin as Anubis commented, "Holy shit, he's a younger version of you."

A twitch of a smile lifted Fury's upper lip. "Every generation needs someone like me. Someone who'll kill without asking questions. He enjoys it. I did, too, at one time." Fury leaned back in his chair.

"We're sure he's not a psychopath?" Anubis leaned forward. "He fronted you. I've never seen that happen."

"He's not a psychopath. Neither am I. We've both been tested. Repeatedly. He has his people. Granted, the ones he … stays around are very few. A damn small pool."

"The others in his class."

"With the exception of Centurion and

Maximus."

"Those two are lone wolves. They didn't go through training with the rest of the class. Do they ever surface? You're their direct contact."

"They exist in the light. We've used each once since they graduated." Fury glanced over at Anubis. "They have lives and day-to-day jobs. When we can't reach the targets any other way, the Council activates them. It's risky."

Anubis nodded. "I can only imagine. Do you think Ice can handle the long ramp-up to this job?"

"He'll do what he's told. He won't like it, but he'll do it."

"And eat Flack out of house and home."

"He won't be there long. Flack and Smith have been working with CCS. They have some ideas. A breadcrumb or two." Fury stood up. "Go make sure he gets tucked in."

"I'll make sure he has a bed and food, but the only one I tuck in is Kadey," Anubis said as he stood.

"Isn't she getting too old for that?" Fury chuckled as they walked out the door.

Anubis smiled and shook his head. "She'll always be my little girl, so … as far as I'm concerned, the answer to that question is no."

CHAPTER 2

Londyn Chatsworth shivered under the watchful lens of the camera. She hated it, hated the son of a bitch who was behind it, and detested her existence on this godforsaken island. Just a year ago, she'd been a successful entrepreneur and influencer on her social media channel. She'd started the cooking and lifestyle channel as a lark. Still, once a semi-famous celebrity mentioned her in an interview, her channel blew up, and she was able to quit her job at the restaurant and devote herself to her channel full-time. She'd had it all. Savings in the bank, a nice place for her and her sister to live, small endorsements with the very real promise of larger opportunities. All because she smiled at the camera and gave practical advice while cooking.

Now, if she never saw another camera, it would be too soon.

"What are you doing?" As her husband's voice came over the speaker, she shuddered with revulsion.

"You're watching me get dressed. Fuck you." Londyn turned her back on the camera and moved across the room. The red light on the camera facing her turned on.

"That's what I'm waiting for." The man's voice rolled out of the speaker.

"When hell freezes over, or you rape my cold, dead body." Londyn would never let that man have her, and for some reason, the bastard *wanted* her to consent. But that didn't mean he didn't abuse her. Taunting him was stupid. She'd push him too far, and he'd lash out. She pulled her long brown hair up into a ponytail.

"I can wait. Can your sister?" The question stilled her in her tracks.

Londyn turned to the camera and put her hands on her hips. "I want to talk to her."

"Submit to me."

"Never."

"Then, no."

The fucker loved the cat-and-mouse game. She shook her head. "How do I know you still have her? How do I know she's safe? How do I know you haven't killed her?" The television in the bedroom turned on, and a video feed of her sister sitting in a bedroom reading a book lit up the screen. Soft music was playing, and she could hear bird songs. Paris's window was open, but the bars on the window made sure she wasn't going anywhere. The date and the time were imprinted on the bottom of the feed.

"Proof enough? Or maybe not." The door to the bedroom slammed open, and Paris jumped up. The book fell to the floor, and her sister shrank to the wall. A man with a gun appeared in the picture and looked up at the camera. "Submit to me, and she's free."

"No." She closed her eyes and shook her head. Her husband was sadistic. If she submitted to him, the game would be over for him. He'd kill her and her sister. Of that, she had no doubt.

"Then you and I will have a meeting tonight. Be prepared and be clean." The television screen turned off, as did the red light on the camera.

Londyn had pushed him too far. She slipped on

a pair of shoes and walked to the kitchen. The state-of-the-art room held every conceivable appliance, and all the equipment was expensive, top-of-the-line products. She made a shopping list for food delivered once a month when the helicopter landed and the guards switched. She'd never seen a guard. The food was left in coolers and bags on the front porch. When she was ordered, she went to the front and retrieved the groceries. If she didn't, well, *that* time he beat her so badly, she broke a molar. He took great joy in pulling what remained of the tooth without any pain reliever. He could have had his way with her, strapped down like she was, but he didn't. He *wouldn't*. Not without her consent. Hurting her? He didn't have a problem with that. While she lay on the floor in pain, he jacked off. He was disgusting, sadistic, and agoraphobic. All she had to do was walk out the door, and he couldn't follow her. His guards would, however. There was no land to be seen from any of the windows. She had no idea how far it was to help. But all of that was moot because Paris was there on that island. If she tried to leave, Paris would pay the price.

She knew the food delivery was coming. After hearing the chopper overhead earlier, she worked to make room for the new food, freezing that which could be saved and cleaning out any bits and pieces that she couldn't use—a function of habit, not necessity. Wasting food should be the least of her concerns, but it was a bit of her past that the bastard couldn't strip from her.

"You may retrieve the food."

She shot the camera a look that could wither a rock and finished what she was doing before she dried her hands and went to the front door. The coolers were the type that could be pulled, thankfully. She hadn't been to the gym in almost a year. God, had it been that long? Londyn could hardly believe it. She was drugged while out with friends and had vague memories of being forced to say I do and thinking it was funny that the minister was on a video camera. The next thing she remembered was waking up in hell. Londyn made several trips to the door and brought in all the groceries before unloading them. A folded piece of paper taped to a spaghetti noodle package she hadn't ordered shocked her.

Londyn glanced up at the camera. The red light glowed brightly. He was watching. Of course, he was. He always watched her. God, she couldn't let him know. She wouldn't. She'd look later when working in the kitchen wouldn't raise suspicion. Londyn put the pasta in the pantry, turning the note to the wall.

Through rote memory, she placed all the other supplies and sundries. Her mind raced with the implication of the white paper. It could be nothing. She told herself that over and over. The store could have taped an inventory tag to the box. However, she *never* ordered pasta. She made her own. It wasn't difficult, and Bruce expected fresh pasta. Bruce. She turned to the camera. "I'm putting the coolers out."

His voice came over the speakers, "Do it."

"Then I'm going out into the garden."

"Be prepared for tonight," her husband warned her again.

"Can I ever be prepared for what you'll do?" she mumbled as she grabbed the cooler.

"Life would be easier if you submitted."

"I'd be dead, though, wouldn't I?" she asked as she wheeled the coolers through the hallway. The red light on the camera by the front door activated.

"Do you think I would?"

Londyn stopped and looked up at the camera. "What?"

"You asked if I'd kill you if you submitted."

"Huh, I said that out loud?" She opened the door and wheeled one and then the other cooler out onto the porch.

"You did. Killing you would be inconvenient at this point."

"Ah, see, that makes me feel so much better," Londyn sneered and headed straight through the great room and into the four-acre garden enclosed by the house. She stepped over the remote-controlled lawn mower and went to the garden's center. Bushes and trees swayed in the breeze, and she sat down underneath the biggest tree with the largest canopy. She could see the building that housed the guards from there. Just the rooftop, but it was enough. That was when she was as close to Paris as she could get.

Londyn put her head on her knees and cried. Bruce Jonas. The bastard. He'd tried to woo her when she'd first arrived at the island. To convince her that having her abducted, drugged, and married against her will was because he was in love with her. He'd seen her channel and decided they were soul mates. She wiped at her tears. When she refused to have sex with him that night, he'd beat her for the first time. He'd dragged her by her hair to the television, and with a few strokes on a tablet that she'd learned he always had with him, Paris's limp body being thrown on that damn bed appeared on the screen. A guard had entered and shaken her sister awake. Paris's scream was something she'd never forget. Londyn was left on the floor, and Paris was left alone in the bedroom. They'd both cried for a long time that night, although Paris had no idea Londyn could see or hear her.

Londyn knew tonight would be bad. It had been a long time, over a month, since Bruce had touched her. *Killing you would be inconvenient at this point.* What did that mean? Would giving in to the son of a bitch free Paris? No. She couldn't see it. Londyn knew his name. She knew what he looked like. Paris didn't, but that didn't mean she hadn't seen other things like the guards' faces. She'd resist the man as long as she could. The only thing she had power over was her submission. If Paris was ever in danger, then and only then would she play that card.

"Time is up. Come back in." The voice echoed through the outdoor speaker by the door. He couldn't see her out there, and she'd never seen him outside, even though the garden was the house's interior. She swiped at her eyes and nose before standing up. Londyn wouldn't make her punishment for pushing him even more extreme.

She paused and looked up at the tree. "God, please. Please help us. Please save us from this monster."

CHAPTER 3

*I*ce watched the woman re-enter the house. From his position in the tree, it would have been hard for her to see him, but not impossible. He'd been watching the bastard and trying to intercept digital signals for over a month. He'd seen the fucker beat the hell out of the woman, and then … Ice rolled his eyes and moved after she was back inside. The little platform he'd built sucked, but it did the job. At night when the lights were turned off, he dropped to the ground and stretched, did a couple hundred push-ups and even some pull-ups on the tree branches. The house was wired. Any sound made inside the structure would be monitored. The garden. Nothing. But he could see why the man wasn't concerned. Unless someone were to climb over the top of the house without being seen by guards, climb up a tree, assemble a platform, and spy on the fucker, the house was secure. *Right.*

The guards were pretty useless. They performed the mandated walks around the island. But as far as they knew, no one entered or exited the private island. Ice snorted soundlessly. He was over the house every night while the guards ate and the target was eating his gourmet food. Man, did it smell good, too. The floor-to-ceiling windows in the kitchen allowed him to watch her cook, and she'd usually open the sliding French doors when she was in the kitchen. The screens kept the bugs out. Smelling that food was torture. Or at least he'd thought it was until that night about a month ago. His fourth night in the tree, as a matter of fact.

Watching what that bastard did to her and not acting was visceral torture. Visceral. Obtained through emotions. Emotions he didn't possess, so in fact, it wasn't torture, but it was a wrong he would correct. Why he wanted to correct it was beyond him. Shit never bothered him. Yet the man's obscene actions did. The woman was strong. She stood her ground, but his target was stronger.

He could hear the man scream at her. He witnessed the threats and the way she squared her shoulders and wouldn't back down. He'd also witnessed her slump in exhaustion, or perhaps resignation, when his target walked away. Inexplicably, he felt a kindred determination with her. They both had to stand up to the vile fuckers of the world. She did it without training, and she'd probably lose. He wouldn't. Especially when he took that monster out.

The woman's plea just then also bothered him … because who in the hell was "us"? *Please protect us.* He hadn't seen another person in the house, and he'd know. The guards occupied the guardhouse, and no, he wasn't stupid enough to try to infiltrate that place. Not that he wouldn't kill every motherfucker over there, but it wasn't sanctioned, and if he went around killing people just because he wanted to, Guardian would probably send one of the ancient ones after him.

Not that he was worried about it. He had no desire to kill for the sake of killing, but the fact that it didn't bother him was what made him so damn good at his job. He didn't like people in general, but the woman needed a protector, and she had none. No husband, no brother, uncle, dad

... Valkyrie would kill him for that list. Females didn't need protectors, according to her. Well, females like Valkyrie didn't. The ones like the one going into the kitchen—she needed help.

He watched her reach into the pantry and turn toward the window. The red dot on the camera came on. Ice glanced to his right. The man was always behind that desk. He watched her every move. What else he did was beyond any of them. He'd go into the room off the office three times a day. Ice couldn't see any windows, so it was probably a secure area. The only computer system he'd seen was the stand-alone system the guy used to monitor the cameras. CCS couldn't log in because it wasn't connected to the internet. Nothing else. No computer, cell phone, or way to communicate with the outside world. Ice tapped out a message each time the man went into the room. It was all he could do. From what Ice could determine, the guy didn't have internet access. He wasn't buying it for a second. Everyone was connected in their day and age. What was in that room? The "us" the woman was talking about?

His phone vibrated, and he pulled it out of his pocket.

· · ·

KRIS MICHAELS

>>>CONFIRMED your location as entity. Proceed with mission. Obtain hardware.

WELL, halle-fucking-lujah. Find and grab whatever stupid computer the man was sending signals with, bag it, and get gone after he slit the guy's throat.

It was damn hard to find him because he didn't move. Didn't spend money they could trace. His only mistake was some kind of video feed about a year ago. That was captured by one of the countries monitoring the abnormalities. When the geeks at CCS finally put two and two together, he landed on a private island off South America. Nice and isolated. A perfect evil scientist compound. Well, evil computer nerd-slash-warlord-slash-plunderer of all things compound.

Info was pinged to him when CCS had any via satellite. Short bursts that couldn't be traced. There was nothing on the guy. Nothing on the ownership of the island. It was purchased, but CCS couldn't find the owner. A series of never-ending moving targets. Shadow type nothing. But Ice knew the man wasn't a shadow for some country or organization. He wasn't a risk to anyone but that woman, and the reason was obvious. The man was agoraphobic. Ice had watched him try to come into the garden. The physical reaction to being close to the door was obvious. Sweat, stomach cramps, pale skin, and shallow breathing. When the man stepped out and literally shit his pants before getting back into the house, there was no doubt he was in his own prison. The question was, why was the woman locked away with him, too?

Agoraphobia was something he'd studied in passing, as had everyone in the classes he'd attended before joining Guardian. Agoraphobia was so much more than what was portrayed in Hollywood bullshit. It seemed like the bastard was a true agoraphobic on top of being some kind of a tech wizard-slash-warlord extraordinaire. At least that was what the Council classified the fucker as since they'd coded him as the entity responsible for the atrocities Ice was shown at the Rose.

He reached into his bag and pulled out a long-lasting sucker. It was long-lasting until he crunched the hell out of the thing. He'd be glad to get back to civilization, to food that didn't come in foil wrappers, and to indoor plumbing.

His eyes wandered back to the woman by the stove. She turned sideways, apparently stirring whatever was in the frying pan, but her free hand unfolded a small piece of paper. He saw her stop stirring, and then she jerked and glanced over her shoulder. Ice watched as the man headed down the hallway toward the kitchen. The woman crumbled up the paper and ... ate it. Holy shit, she ate the paper.

The man stopped in the doorway. He couldn't hear the words exchanged, but the woman shook her head. The man pointed at her, and he imagined the words weren't polite. The woman shrunk under his words, whatever they were. Ice couldn't wait to kill the guy. Tonight, after the guards were done with their rounds for the night. It couldn't be soon enough.

* * *

ICE CLOSED his eyes and shook his head. He could hear the bastard hurting the woman. He glanced at his watch. He couldn't move until the fucking guards were done for the night. The house was a glass box, and a casual glance from a bored guard on the way back to the house they occupied would endanger the mission.

He dropped to the ground and worked the kinks out of his muscles, watching the house while he prepared to take the bastard out. Movement caught his eye, and he froze. A guard peered in the front window just as his target pulled the woman by her hair into his office. She was limp. The target flopped the woman's hand out and stepped on her fingers, grinding down on them with the heel of his shoe. Ice ran to the back of the house and entered through the kitchen. He moved along the hallway to where he could see into the study.

The woman woke, screaming. His target kicked her when she tried to pull her hand out from under his foot. Her head flung backward, and a burst of red painted the man's khaki pants. *The son of a bitch.* Ice wasn't one to torture when he killed, but damn it, that guy deserved to be skinned alive.

Ice used a mirror in his hand to see the window and the guard. The guard's face loomed large in the window. Pocketing the mirror, he moved forward, sinking beside a wide credenza in the foyer. From there, he could see the guards and the study. A hand on the guard's shoulder turned him. Ice dipped below the wood cabinet, making sure he wasn't seen. He glanced back up, watched as the guards spoke, and then turned again to the window. *Come on. Leave. Damn it.* Ice thought as he heard his target scream, "Submit to me!"

The woman mumbled something, but obviously, it wasn't what the man wanted to hear. Ice glanced up at the window. The guards hadn't left. His target stomped out of the room, past him and the guards heading down the hall. The woman scurried toward the desk. Ice shook his head, trying to understand what she was doing. On her knees, she pulled one of the desk drawers out.

Ice glanced back. The guards had disappeared. They'd probably freaked about being seen. He needed them to stay gone. He moved forward, trying to find the woman. She wasn't by the desk any longer. Ice pushed back into the hall off the office when he heard the bastard jogging back to the study. The target skidded to a stop, a thick leather strap in his hand. Ice moved to see what was happening. The woman pulled out a pistol and aimed it at the man with one hand. The other she placed under the one supporting the gun without using it to grip the weapon. Her hand was so swollen that supporting her gun hand was all it could do.

He could see the fear in her eyes. He could sense that she wouldn't pull that damn trigger. The woman would die. His target would beat her to death, of that he was certain. Not on his watch.

That fucker didn't get to hurt her any more. She'd paid enough. "No," Ice said to himself, lifting from where he was crouched. Simultaneously, his target snarled and lifted the strap. Ice moved into position and, with the practiced ease of hundreds of thousands of throws, launched a tomahawk through the air. He used enough force to drive the three-inch double-bladed head, twelve-inch-long tactical axe through muscle and bone.

The man jerked, dropping the strap, and reached to his back, clawing at the axe buried there. His legs collapsed under him, but the bastard didn't give, and obviously, the axe hadn't buried deep enough to kill the fuck. Ice moved forward, grabbed the man's head, pulled it backward, and slit his throat.

A gasp from the woman brought his attention from the man to her. She was still pointing the weapon, but now, it was pointed at him. Ice lifted his hand, and his target's head hit the marble floor with a resounding thunk. "I'm not here to hurt you."

"I was going to kill him." The gun shook violently in the woman's hands.

Ice nodded. "Yeah, I saw. You don't need his blood on your hands. Give me that gun, okay?"

The woman looked at him, and he winced. The bruise on her cheek where the fucker kicked her was already green and purple. Her eye was swelling. He moved forward a few inches. "Let me have the gun?"

"He has Paris." The woman continued to point the gun right at him. Ice cocked his head. The safety was on. He nodded.

"Who's Paris?" He moved forward and took the weapon from her hand, putting the gun in one of his cargo pockets.

"My sister. I got a note today. It was with the groceries. There's a guard who'll keep her safe. He said she'd be okay and to do what I needed to do to get away." The woman dropped to her butt. "I was going to kill him."

"You didn't." Ice glanced back at his target. "Does he have a computer?" The woman blinked and turned toward the room where Ice had seen him disappear. He spun and trotted to the door. "Fuck." *Biometrics*. He glanced at the dead man on the floor. "We need to put him on ice. Where's the closest bathtub?"

The woman's brow furrowed. "What?"

Okay, he'd give her that. It was a weird fucking question. "This door is controlled by biometrics. I don't know if the computers inside are controlled by them, too." He pulled his tomahawk out of Bruce's back, lifted the bastard, peeling his eyelid open, and moved the dead weight to the scanner. It was a struggle to keep the man's head level. Ice jammed his knee up under the man's crotch and lifted with his arms and his leg. The computer screen flashed green, the lock snapped clear of the deadbolt, and the door opened. Ice dropped the dead man, then peered into the room. There were fifteen doors to small, dome-like structures. He stepped over the dead man and walked into the room. Carefully, he opened one of the domes and blinked. The tech surrounding the computer system was beyond anything he'd ever seen or been briefed on. Shutting the door, he glanced at the nomenclature above each door. It was way beyond his pay grade, and he was at the top of that structure.

"I'm not a computer geek, but I know shielded hubs when I see them. I need to get someone out here to look at these computers," Ice groaned. Now, he was talking to himself. He'd spent way too much time up in that fucking tree. He grabbed his target and looked back at the woman. "Nearest bathtub?" The woman tried to stand but fell back to the floor. "Whoa, just stay right there. I'll help you as soon as I get him iced down."

"To the right. Who are you?" The woman stared at him.

"Someone who heard your prayer earlier," Ice said as he picked up the target and headed in the direction she'd indicated. He kicked two doors open before finding the bathroom. He dropped the bastard from his shoulder into the tub, then jogged back to the den. "Ice?"

"Kitchen. There's an under-counter unit." She pointed, but he knew where that was. He flew into the kitchen, keeping the lights off in case the Peeping Tom guard decided to return. He opened the pantry door and searched for a garbage bag. Finding one, he filled the black plastic with ice and carried it to the bathtub, pouring it over the fucker.

He filled two more bags, icing his target down before returning to the study. The woman was cleaning up the blood with towels. "You don't need to do that."

"Are you taking us with you when you leave?" She rolled a blood-soaked towel into a dry one.

Ice blinked at that. Hell, he had no idea. His mission had morphed. "I don't have any answers right now. I need to make contact with my superiors." He pulled out his phone and hit the number that would take him to Guardian.

"Operator Two Seven Four. Standby Sunset Operative Sixteen."

Ice paced as he watched the woman clean up the blood. "Authenticate Snow." Fury's voice cracked over the connection.

"Frozen."

"Status?"

"Target is terminated. Biometrics on the computer room. The woman living here with him—"

"He kidnapped my sister and me." The hatred in the woman's voice snapped his attention to her.

"Okay." Ice nodded at her. "His prisoner and her sister need airlift."

"Guards?"

"Housed in a large building to the east of the main building. By my count, there are twelve guards. Five on the day shift and five on the night shift. Two never leave the house."

"That's because they're guarding my sister."

Fury cussed and then said, "Standby."

"Just what I want to do," Ice mumbled. He glanced down at the petite woman. Her face was a mess, her hand swollen from being stepped on, yet she was cleaning up after the fucker. Ice took a breath and looked away. The woman was something. He was right; she had steel in her backbone. Not enough to kill his target, but enough to survive. He respected that. Hell, he applauded it. That steel kept her alive. He knew how that worked. People weren't born with that trait; it was formed through fire. He'd walked through it and so had she.

He listened to nothing on the phone and turned back toward her. Damn, she'd taken some hard blows. "We need to get you cleaned up and some ice on your face and hand." The woman reached up to her cheek but stopped when she saw the blood on her hands.

"Please, can you get Paris out of there?"

Ice stared at the fear and desperation in the woman's eyes. "I—"

"Get her sister," Fury's voice commanded in his ear.

Ice jerked his attention back to the ancient one. "You do realize that means I'm going to take on twelve guards, right?"

"Are you afraid to get your hands dirty?" Fury taunted.

"Ah, no. I just don't want to get them slapped." He had zero problems taking out the fuckers who kept the woman and her sister captive.

"Do what you have to do. Can you disassemble the computer systems?"

"Can we go to video?" Ice said. "I'll show you what I'm working with." The camera activated, and he turned the phone, placing it in front of him as he walked to the computer room door he'd propped open.

"You getting this?"

"I am," a female's voice spoke over the connection. Ice frowned but kept moving forward. He gave them a long look at the biometrics outside the door before stepping into the room. He turned the camera so they could get a look at everything.

"What do you think?" He turned the screen toward himself, and his eyebrows popped up. The connection had dropped. He walked out of the room, and his cell phone started vibrating.

"The room is shielded." The woman's voice came across the connection before he could speak. "Get closer to the door. Can you open the door to one of those hubs?"

The woman limped over to him. "I can do it."

She limped past him and opened a door with her good hand.

"Rose, we're going to need to get someone down there. That's advanced tech. If they take it apart, it could erase any evidence on the system. Wait, holy shit. My facial rec system is freaking out …"

Ice signaled for the woman to come out. She limped to the door and looked up at him, then asked, "You're going to help us?"

He stared down at her and nodded. "I'll get your sister out of there."

She closed her eyes and seemed to cave in around herself. "Thank you. You're American, right? Are you with the CIA or something? I know you weren't looking for us."

"Yeah, I'm with the "or something" company." Ice hedged his answer.

"Ice, the woman with you, what's her name? Never mind, put me on speaker, please." The woman's voice came across the connection loud enough for both of them to hear. He hit the button, and the woman on the other end of the line repeated her question.

"I'm Londyn Chatsworth. My sister Paris and I were taken by men who work for Bruce Jonas, and they drugged me, then forced me to marry him."

"Wait, that was your husband?" Ice pointed toward the bathroom.

"Hush, Ice. Londyn, would you please spell his name for me?" The woman shushed him, which … wow, that hadn't happened since he was maybe six?

Londyn spelled out the name and then looked at him, answering his questions. "According to the law, yes. We were married online. I can remember that much. I wasn't even in the same room as him or the minister. He showed me the document. It's my signature. I don't remember signing it, though. The document is in the safe in his office. After it happened, the world went black again. The next memory I have is waking up here." The woman's chin lifted. "I never slept with him. That's why he beat me," she whispered to him as if he needed that information. Well, good for her, but damn, the fucker should have never been able to put her in that position.

"Gees Louise, Pete, and repeat! There's a nationwide search for her and her sister. Londyn's internet famous. Just doing a law enforcement search on your name has alarms going off across the country." The phone muffled as the woman

43

asked, "Babe, could you get Ethan to shut those down?" She was back loud and clear with, "It's a huge missing person's case. Wait, I have the date she went missing. You said you were married online?"

"Yes. I was still wearing the clothes I was in at the nightclub. Someone had to have slipped something into my drink." The woman slumped against the wall. Ice wanted to gather her in his arms and keep her from harm, but he'd already done that, hadn't he? He'd killed the monster who had taken her. Not an intentional enough act, if you ask him. Those other fuckers in the guardhouse would pay for being accomplices to the vulgarity.

"Enough chitchat," Fury interrupted. "Ice, get the sister. Stand by at your location for incoming tech support. When will the next rotation of guards or supplies come to the island?"

"Not for thirty days," the woman responded before Ice could.

"Are there any other personnel who come to the island?"

"Three times since I've been here. Everyone is always helicoptered in. I was locked in the room. I didn't know who was there, but I could hear voices. Men and women."

"Ma'am, we aren't there to rescue you or your sister, but we will protect you and get you off the island. We'll need you and your sister to sign a non-disclosure statement. Nothing you saw during your time on the island or events preceding it can be discussed publicly or privately. To do so would jeopardize your and your sister's safety. The events you are involved in are too complicated to explain, but it's a matter of national security."

Ice watched the woman's face as yet another person entered the conversation. He recognized the voice. The big man. CEO and all that shit. Somehow the parameters of the mission he'd started months ago had morphed during the time it took to track down the bastard. Ice didn't usually give a fuck what was happening outside his job, but the lady deserved answers.

"I'll sign anything. I don't want to talk about what's happened in the last year." Londyn shifted her gaze from the phone to him. "Please, bring Paris to me."

"Ice, take the phone off the speaker," the boss of the organization commanded.

Ice did as commanded and walked away from the woman. "You rang?"

"The guards are considered unavoidable collateral damage. Get the other woman out safely. They are American citizens. Until our tech unit gets there, keep them together and safe. No communications off that island."

"I understand," he acknowledged.

"Good work. Archangel Out."

"CCS is out," the woman signed off.

"Don't drop your guard. We don't know the impact taking this guy out will produce. Ripples aren't good because the epicenter is right where you are," Fury said.

"Understood. I've never asked this before, but who in the hell is this guy?" Ice could feel those ripples floating out from that island as if they were a physical thing.

"I'll let you know when I can." Fury paused. "You'll be there until tech gets every bit of data from those machines."

"Guards will change out in thirty days."

"I'm aware. We'll send in reinforcements if we need to stay longer."

"And the women?"

"Are staying with you."

"Why? They don't know anything."

"She's his wife. She now owns that island, giving us the right to be there. It untangles many wires."

"They need to go home."

"No. Coming back here would release a media frenzy. I don't care if she understands or not. They stay until all of us leave that island."

"And the dead men?"

"Shark bait."

"I like the way you think."

"Because we think alike. The Rose is out."

Ice turned around and headed back into the study. Londyn was on her knees cleaning the floor.

"I'm going to go get your sister. I need you to go to a safe place and lock yourself in. I don't want someone to slip through my fingers and use you as leverage."

Londyn frowned. "All the doors lock from the outside."

Ice glanced at the locks and realized what she said was true. "Then find a closet they wouldn't look in. Get in it. Don't come out until you hear your sister calling for you."

Londyn looked at the floor and slowly started to stand. Ice reached out to help her up, and she let him take some of her weight. "Thank you. It's been a long time since anyone has ..."

The woman teared up, and Ice wasn't too sure

what to do. He tapped her arm with his hand, hopefully in a comforting motion. Hell, the only person he'd ever comforted was Brooke, and that was because he was wrapped around that kid's finger. Not as bad as Reaper and Malice, but yeah, he was tangled up around that little digit. "You have to be strong, just for a bit longer. Go, grab a bag of ice for that hand and cheek, then get into a closet and stay there until you hear Paris." Ice felt a bit wound around a finger right now. Like the sensation he got around Brooke, yet different. With Londyn there was a stark difference, and that was something he didn't know how to process. Yet.

She nodded and started to limp away. "Wait. A guard is helping her. Manuel is his name."

Ice nodded. He didn't know what would happen at the guardhouse. If the guard advanced against him, he'd be marked as an enemy. "Go. I'll get your sister."

She stared at him for a moment and then nodded her head. "He has more bullets for the gun. In the desk drawer."

Ice smiled. "I won't need them." Guns were not his weapon of choice. His trusty axe and knives were more than enough. Quiet, deadly, and up close and personal.

She blinked at him as if trying to figure out what he would do. Finally, she nodded and limped down the hall. He waited until she turned into the kitchen before sprinting out to the tree, pulling down his kit, and loading up. Ice unwrapped a small sucker, popped it in his mouth, and left the garden like he did every other night. Up and over the house, across the roof and down the other side. He landed lightly on his feet and rolled his shoulders. Turning his head, he zeroed in on the lights coming from the house about a quarter mile from where he stood. He pulled his black silk ski mask out of his pocket and pulled it over his blond hair, careful to avoid the stick of his sucker. His gloves went on next. They kept his grip solid when blood ran down the blades.

Ice turned and walked toward the house. This night, blood would flow, and Ice relished the thought.

CHAPTER 4

*I*ce watched as two of the twelve men walked down to the beach and lit up. He moved around and came up from the dark side of the beach, where the house's exterior lights didn't illuminate the ground.

"I'm telling you, Manuel will be a problem." The man took a long draw on his cigarette. Ice stilled, willing to listen to what the two had to say about Manuel. Ice was wagering fifty-fifty that Manuel would be alive at the end of the night.

"He's in love with the girl."

"Fuck, who isn't? She's pretty. Leave it alone. Nothing will come of it. Besides, he's fucking her, who cares?" The two men laughed.

"I don't know. Seems like the boss would be

pissed, but that's on Manuel. Whatever. I come out here for thirty days, relax, and get paid. I don't care if that girl ever leaves that room."

The other man took a deep pull on his cigarette and blew it out before he spoke. "Ah, she'll get out. The boss will replace the first one with this one. He's done it before. Sooner or later, he'll snap, and that one will die. His anger. He'll kill her. Usually, before this amount of time has passed."

The other one lit another cigarette from his first one. "He's done this before?"

"Yes, but never with an American. He always has one in waiting. But this one, the one in the house, she's different. I think he loves her."

"Yeah, well, his love language is pretty fucking weird. He was beating the shit out of her tonight. I pulled Manuel away when I saw the boss heading out in a rage. We'll probably have to get rid of the body in the morning. No one can survive after being beaten with a strap like that. He was so pissed he didn't see us at the window. Thank God. You should get some rest. I'll take over and have a few words with Manuel. By morning, you won't have to worry about that woman in the guard-house again. The other one will be dead, and he'll want this one taken to the main house."

"If only," the other man chuffed.

Ice moved over several rocks and crouched down as he approached, shielding himself from view by using one guard to block the other's vision. With a hatchet in one hand and a long blade in the other, Ice attacked. The pick end of the hatchet went around the neck of the guard with his back to Ice. Ice pulled it back and to the side. As the surprised man was flung away with a gaping hole in his neck, Ice buried the long knife into the upper belly of the other guard facing him. He lifted with all his might and twisted the knife. The guard dropped; his heart punctured by the sharp steel.

Two down. Ten to go. Ice walked up from the beach. There was no movement in the house. He strode up the steps and walked into the building. Three men were in the living room watching television. Ice didn't break stride, grabbing the head of the man on the couch and slitting his throat before throwing his hatchet at the guard who could see him. The guard on the chair was sprayed with blood from the man Ice had almost decapitated. That stunned him long enough for Ice to walk over to the couch, drop on the man, and shove his knife through the bottom of his jaw and straight into his brain.

Ice jogged over to the man he'd axed and stepped on his face to dislodge the hatchet that had split his forehead. Fucking missed his mark, which pissed him off. The sound of bone against metal as he worked the hatchet out couldn't be heard over the television. Five down. Seven to go. Ice didn't try to hide the sound of his footfalls. He walked back to where he'd heard men talking. Turning the corner into the kitchen, he threw the hatchet at the man who turned from the refrigerator. That bastard landed perfectly. He swung to his right, the grip of his knife facing backward—the blade buried in a man's chest. The ribs diverted the knife upward, and the guy dropped. The third man raised his gun simultaneously as Ice pulled his Ka-Bar from its sheath and let it fly. The gun clattered to the floor as the man gripped the knife planted firmly in his chest. Ice lunged forward and dropped the big guy with a flying kick. He pulled out the knife and slit his throat. Some guys didn't get the message to die with the first blade. Eight out of twelve were down.

"Hey, keep it quiet down there. I'm trying to sleep up here!" someone yelled from upstairs.

Ice rolled his eyes and retrieved his weapons. "Hey, Louis? Dave?" the man called, and Ice moved out into the hallway. A guy dressed in boxer briefs came down the stairs. His hair stuck straight up, and he looked grumpy as hell as he walked straight to the living room. Ice jumped him from the back and dropped to the floor as his knife obliterated the muscle and cartilage connecting his head to his body. Nine down.

Ice made his way upstairs. Number ten was asleep in bed. He'd never wake up. Eleven walked out of a room at the same time as Ice left his last victim. The gun was up, and a shot rang out. Ice rolled, but not away from the man, toward him. He lifted in a practiced maneuver and thrust his long knife into the man's gut, slicing him open. The warmth of the man's organs against his hand told him when to retract the knife. The strangled scream didn't matter. There was only one more, and Ice was ready to kill Satan tonight. Leaving the eviscerated man to die, he moved down the hall. A door with a clasp and lock hanging from it told him where Paris was. It also told him that the last man had her hostage.

Ice lifted his foot and kicked in the door. A man stood with a gun pointed at Ice and the younger version of Londyn clinging to his side. "I don't know who you are, but I'll kill you if you try to hurt her."

Ice sneered. "If I wanted to kill you, you'd be dead, Manuel."

The man blinked, and the woman opened her eyes. She gasped and asked, "Did Londyn send you?"

"Paris, go straight outside and run to the big house. The front door isn't locked. Go in and call for Londyn." Ice wasn't giving her a choice in the matter, and he needed to determine whether Manuel would be a liability or an asset. He didn't give a flying fuck either way.

Paris stepped in front of Manuel. "He's protected me. He's taking me out of here."

Manuel placed a hand on her shoulder. "Paris, go to your sister. The two of us need to come to an agreement."

Paris looked up at Manuel. "Manny, please ..."

He smiled at her. "Go."

She glanced at Ice and then walked toward the door. Ice growled, "Run, don't look anywhere but toward that big house."

He heard Paris's gasp as she entered the hall-way. "Run!" Manuel yelled. The sound of the woman's feet on the stairs and then the foyer echoed up to them. When the sound of her running was gone, Manuel tossed his weapon to the bed. "Kill me. As long as she's safe, I'm okay."

Ice lifted his knife and hatchet. The congealed blood turned the metal red. "Know this. I will kill you if anything you tell me is false." Ice stared at the man, who paled yet stood strong. Saying you were willing to die and facing death were two different things. "How long have you worked for that fucker?"

"Two rotations on this island. This is my third. I've hired a ship's captain to leave a skiff on the island's far side. I would kill every last one of the bastards I work with to get her off the island safely. I knew what the man was doing to her sister. I wanted to stop it tonight, but then no one would be left to protect Paris." The man sighed. "It was a no-win situation. But I would have taken her sister out of here, too. The boss can't leave the house."

"And he would have called in reinforcements. They would have captured you and the women. A stupid idea." Ice cocked his head. "Valiant, but stupid."

The man shook his head. "It was all I could do.

It was a *chance*. Eventually, he would have killed both of them. The men here talk about his sick ways and that he's gone through at least a dozen women."

"Where are the weapons kept?"

"There's an armory in the basement. Harold has the keys. I've only been in there once when I first started working here. When unscheduled helicopter visits happen, we're given M4s and put on lookout."

"Did you see who came to the island?"

"No. But it was a big helicopter, like the kind we fly in on. It could hold twelve." Manuel looked past him. "Are they all dead?"

"Dead or dying." Ice didn't drop his gaze. "Why risk your life for the girl?"

Manuel's face softened. "We talked for hours through the door. Whispering all night long when it was my shift to watch her. She's special. She couldn't be sacrificed to that monster. I couldn't let it happen."

"Do you have any weapons on you?" Ice hadn't relaxed an iota, and he wouldn't.

"I have a knife in my boot and another Beretta in a belt holster at my back," Manuel answered, then turned around. Ice carefully slid his long knife into its sheath, then pulled Manuel's weapon from the holster.

"Take out the knife with your left hand." Most people hadn't spent years perfecting a throw from both hands like he had. Besides, with his back to Ice, the man would have to turn to throw. Seconds he'd use to kill the fucker.

"How do you know I'm right-handed?" Manuel asked as he slowly lowered his left hand, keeping his right raised.

"You threw the weapon onto the bed with your right hand, and your weapon in your belt was positioned for a right-handed draw." Simplistic shit that people who weren't in the business of assassination would miss.

The knife came out slowly and was tossed onto the bed. "Are you going to kill me?"

Ice narrowed his eyes and felt a sneer spread across his face. "I haven't decided. Turn around." Manuel did as instructed, with his hands still held high in the air. He nodded toward the door. "Take me to the communications room."

"There isn't one." Manuel frowned. "We're searched before getting on the helicopter. Harold has a radio that he gets from the person he relieves. It goes to the boss and only the boss. He has an earpiece the entire time he's on the island in case the boss wants something. We watch movies we bring to the island on the television and listen to the radio. That's it. No internet, no phones."

"What do you do if someone is hurt or sick?"

"I don't know. It's never happened." Manuel shrugged, his hands lowering, but from fatigue, not from a ploy. Ice saw when the guard realized it, pushing them higher into the air.

"We're going to the main house."

"Can I ask who you are? I can tell you're American. Are you with the military or something?"

Ice narrowed his eyes. "Or something. Move, or I'll kill you. It doesn't matter to me." He was tired of talking.

Manuel's eyes popped open, and he stepped out of the room. Ice heard the soft moan of the man he gutted. Manuel stepped over the man, but Ice didn't. "Stop," he instructed Manuel. Ice used the back hook of his hatchet and ripped the man's throat open. Killing wasn't about torture. He'd needed to move quickly when he'd dropped the man. Now, he could finish the task.

Manuel looked back over his shoulder. "Jesus."

"Nope, not even in your wildest dreams," Ice

said and stood up. "Move down the stairs and out of the house."

Manuel followed directions but saw the men in the living room. "They're all dead?"

"Everyone but you," Ice confirmed.

Once they reached and entered the main house, Paris ran to Manuel. He dropped his arms to catch her and immediately threw them up in the air again.

Ice moved to the side and took off his ski mask. "You can put them down."

Londyn limped over to where they were. "Thank you for taking care of my sister."

Manuel held Paris and nodded at Londyn. "I wish I could have stopped him tonight."

Londyn turned her gaze to Ice. "Someone did." She blinked at him. "You need a shower."

Ice had no doubt he was covered in blood. To let his guard down, he'd need to make sure there were no hostiles, and he wasn't sure about Manuel yet.

"Yeah. I need to lock him in a room."

"What? Why?" Paris shouted.

"Because he doesn't trust me. It's all right. I get it." Manuel dropped a kiss on the top of Paris's head. "You're safe. He could lock me in a box, and I'd be okay with it."

"Then put me in the room with him," Paris pleaded as she grabbed Manuel's hand.

"Paris." Londyn sighed and looked at Ice. "Please. She trusts him."

"Happy for her. I don't, and I won't gamble your life or mine. He goes into a room while I get cleaned up. I'll spring him when I'm done." Ice couldn't give either woman more than that.

"I'll be fine." Manuel tipped Paris's chin up. "He's here to protect you. I'll take all the help I can get."

"Let's go."

Manuel moved down the hallway as Paris and Londyn watched. Ice stopped at the bathroom. The windows were solid glass brick. "In there."

Manuel walked in and stopped. "The boss?"

"Wouldn't want you to be lonely." Ice shut the door, turned the key on the outside lock, and pocketed the piece of brass.

"You can use his room. He has clothes you could wear," Londyn said when he reached the foyer. Paris glared daggers at him, but he didn't give a shit.

"How's your hand?"

Londyn lifted it. "Not as bad as it could be." The swollen fingers had a blue and green tinge. She moved them slowly in and out. "I don't think anything is broken."

"Are there any other guns in the house?"

"No. Well, maybe in the safe, but I don't have the combination," Londyn answered.

"Why? Are we in danger? Is someone coming? The guards?" Paris asked, panicking.

"He just wants to know so he can keep us safe. Right, Ice?"

Ice snapped his attention to Londyn. Ah, the woman who hushed him had said his name, hadn't she? "Correct."

"Ice? What kind of name is that?" Paris looked between him and Londyn, her voice rising an octave.

Londyn smiled and hugged her sister. "What kind of names are Paris and Londyn? We shouldn't poke fun at people's names." Paris started to laugh, but it turned into sobs. Londyn held her sister as tears streamed from her own eyes. "It's okay now, sweetie. It's okay. We're going to be fine." She looked up at Ice. Her eyes secretly begged him to confirm her words.

"You're safe. I'll be back."

He left the women and moved through the house to good ol' Bruce's room. He turned on the shower, stripped off his gloves, then got naked and walked to the closet with his hatchet and knife. He threw open the door and found a pair of jeans he could wear. After grabbing a white button-down, he headed back into the bathroom.

"Oh, I'm sorry."

Ice spun. Londyn was at the bedroom door. "Something wrong?" Ice was immediately on alert.

"Ah, no. I brought towels. Clean towels." She lifted the white terrycloth in her hands. The woman didn't blush, nor did she look away.

"You can leave them in here." He turned and went to the shower with his weapons.

"Do you always shower with them?"

"Only when I'm on a mission." Which wasn't far from the truth. He put the weapons down within easy reach, grabbed the soap, and lathered up.

"Thank you."

Ice opened his eyes and stared at Londyn, who was leaning against the doorway and looking straight at him. He continued to wash as he watched her. She turned to the mirror and looked at herself. "I know we weren't your mission. I don't know if I could have pulled the trigger tonight."

Ice shut off the water and opened the glass shower door. She handed him a towel, and he dried off. "You wouldn't have," Ice said. "He would have lashed out with the strap, and you would have flinched."

Londyn turned to him. "I think you're right. So, you saved my life."

Ice put on the jeans commando and grabbed the shirt. "I didn't kill him for you. He was my target." He didn't want her to get any pie-in-the-sky thoughts about him. "I'm not nice and rarely do things for others."

Londyn leaned back against the vanity. "You saved Paris, and you didn't kill Manuel."

"I was told to rescue your sister and kill all the guards on the island. Manuel is a liability."

"He loves her."

"A liability doesn't mean he isn't a good man. A liability means he's an unknown."

"So, Paris and I are liabilities?"

"Until you became part of my mission, yes." Ice dried off his weapons and grabbed his black combat pants. They were soaked in blood, but he needed the pistol and the key.

"Ice?"

He looked up at her.

"You know every key is the same, right? I could have opened the door to the bathroom with any of the other keys. Paris doesn't know. Neither does Manuel."

"Why are you telling me?"

"I'm not a liability." She lifted off the vanity. "I'm a strong woman who has had a year to decide she won't be a victim again. I trust you because of your actions. Perhaps you could trust me because of mine." She turned and limped past him out of the bedroom.

A twitch of a smile hit the side of his lip. Damned if she didn't remind him a bit of Valkyrie.

CHAPTER 5

$\mathcal{L}$ ondyn found Paris sitting outside the bathroom door. "He'll be out soon. I'm going to fix some food." It was what she did when she was nervous or upset.

"I'm staying here," Paris said. "He stayed with me."

"I know." Paris had told her about Manuel after they'd hugged and cried. Londyn was worried, too. Stockholm syndrome was a real thing. She didn't suffer it with Bruce, but was Paris suffering delusions about her guard because of what had transpired over the last year, or had they fallen in love because of those same situations? The fact that Manuel could sneak in a message was his only plus in her thoughts.

Londyn took out a frying pan and two dozen eggs. Her left hand was sore, but if she babied it, it would get stiff, so she worked with it the best she could.

"Food?" Ice asked as he walked into the kitchen.

"Omelets. Do you want one?"

"Three," Ice said and went to the refrigerator, getting a water bottle out.

"A three-egg omelet," Londyn confirmed with a nod.

"No, three omelets. I haven't eaten real food in a month." Ice downed the water bottle and opened the cabinet where the trash compactor was stored.

"How did you know ..." Londyn looked at the cabinet.

"I've been on this island, in that tree, for over a month."

Londyn looked out the dark window toward the green space. "You watched?"

"And waited. I arrived just before he beat you the last time." Ice closed the compactor.

"You watched my bedroom?"

"No. He was my target. I kept a watch on him."

She could see Ice in the reflection of the window. He crossed his arms and stared at her back. Londyn turned and said, "He always watched." She looked up at the camera in the corner of the room. "Always."

"He's dead. He won't watch you ever again."

"No one will. I'll never step in front of a camera again." Her hands shook. "I used to let people into my home, into my life. I had a channel. I cooked and talked about lifestyles and organizational hacks. Things that were interesting to me. That's where he found me. It's why Paris was here. Never again."

Ice stood silent for a long moment. "Technology can be used for good and for evil. Turning your back won't make it go away. Learn to protect yourself. If you don't want to do what you were doing, fine, but pretending tech isn't out there and can't be used against you is stupid."

Londyn blinked. "Did you just call me stupid?" She'd just survived hell, and he called her stupid?

"No. I said turning your back on tech was. I won't sugarcoat the truth. If you want platitudes and Kumbaya shit, I'm not that person."

She couldn't stop the tears. "I don't want platitudes. I want someone to give a shit."

Ice cocked his head. "What?"

"We were taken from our lives. We were

abused." She swiped at the tears. "I don't need plat-itudes, Ice. I need you to give a shit about me. About my sister. Not because we're your mission, but because you're a human being, and so are we."

Ice turned and walked toward the door. He paused for a moment before turning around. His words were low and flat as he spoke, "I watched that man hurt you and then jack off over you. I could do *nothing* about it. I don't feel anger, anxi-ety, or most other emotions. But I wanted to see that man punished for what he did to you. Those types of thoughts are the last thing I need in my line of work or my life, but it's there. Never fucking doubt it." He turned and walked toward the side of the house where he'd locked Manuel.

Londyn leaned against the counter, her heart hammering in her chest. Ice, her savior, and by all accounts, a man sent to kill by some government agency, wanted vengeance for her. Why that was so damn important, she didn't know. She also didn't know why she could still picture his body in that shower. He was impressively built, wide shoulders, narrow waist, and strong legs. Londyn shook her head. But it was his eyes that were the most vivid in her mind's eye. Intense and penetrating, they reached into her soul. She closed her eyes. Right. The day had been overwhelming.

Redirecting her thoughts, Londyn moved methodically. When Paris, Manuel, and Ice returned, she put one foot in front of the other and cooked. There was no sense of overwhelming relief. They were still on the island. Her dead husband was in the bathtub down the hall. No one spoke. Paris held Manuel's hand as if he were her life preserver, and he probably was.

Ice was by Londyn's side, looking at her as if he'd asked her a question. She blinked at him. "What?"

"Do you need help?" He pointed at the bowl she was cracking eggs into.

"Ah …" The offer stopped her. She looked from the eggs to the bowl. "I …" Londyn dropped the egg in her hand. The shell broke, and the inside spread across the floor. Londyn bent down to clean it up but started crying. She couldn't hold back the sobs. Her life, imploded and exploited, abused and captive, cracked like that egg. She sat down on the floor and wrapped herself in a huddle.

A strong hand held her shoulder, and she

turned toward the warmth. "I'm sorry," she repeated the words. She was sorry for the channel, for exposing Paris to that bastard, for being unable to kill him, and for dropping the stupid egg.

When she could control herself, she wiped her tears and nose with her shirt. Gross, but so was running snot. Londyn lifted her head. Across the floor, Paris and Manuel were sitting, and Paris was crying, too. "He hurt you, didn't he? He was the one who did that to your face and hand."

Londyn shook her head, but Ice, who was holding her shoulder, interrupted. "He beat her. He abused her mentally and physically. You weren't the only one who suffered."

Paris crawled over to her. "I didn't know. I'm so sorry."

Londyn held her little sister and stroked her long brown hair. "It's all right. It's all right."

"No, it isn't," Ice said from beside them. "Don't pretend this didn't happen. Deal with it now, be honest with each other, or it will eat at you until it festers and putrefies."

"They didn't hurt you?" Londyn held her sister's head in her hands gently.

"No. I was just alone. Until Manuel started

working with them. I was so scared. Who was it that hurt you?"

"His name was Bruce Jonas."

"Why did he do this?" Paris leaned her head against Londyn's shoulder.

"He was sick." Londyn didn't have any other answer. "But he's gone now."

"Where?" Paris jolted. "Can he come back? Can he find us again?" Paris looked back to Manuel. "He can't, can he?"

"He's dead," Ice said quietly.

Paris turned to look at Ice. She stared at him for several long moments before looking back at Londyn. "I'm not sorry he's dead. I'm not. There isn't anything inside me that feels bad for him."

"I know." Londyn nodded. "Ice will take care of us until we leave the island."

"I can't go back to the apartment, Londyn. I can't. They broke in and took me from the apartment." Paris shook her head. "I don't ever want to go back to someplace he'd know where to look for me."

"He's dead," Londyn repeated the words Ice had said. "He can't hurt us anymore."

"I'm not going back there." Paris shook her head.

"You don't have to." Ice got up. "You can go wherever you want. Start over. Your sister is probably pretty fucking rich."

"What do you mean?" Paris looked up at him.

"She was married to him. He owned this. Money." He shrugged and grabbed a paper towel, wetting it before he stooped down and wiped up the egg.

"Married?"

Londyn nodded. "I don't know why. I was drugged. I remember flashes of the ceremony over a video connection. He showed me the marriage certificate. It looked official."

"I don't understand," Paris whispered.

"Neither do I." Londyn sighed and hugged her sister. She didn't understand any of it.

Ice moved about the kitchen. "Manuel, get off your ass and help with this." Ice flicked the knife he took from the butcher block toward the eggs.

The man got up, but Londyn shook her head. "I can do it."

"You can move, but I'm cooking." Ice went to the fridge and pulled out some bacon. "Chop that into small squares and fry it up on that stove over there." He pointed to the secondary work-station.

"Still don't trust me?" Manuel said as he took the bacon over to the other side of the kitchen.

Ice snorted, "Not as far as I can throw you, and since you're a big fuck, you get the drift."

Paris whispered, "He's really abrupt."

Londyn nodded. That was why she liked him. She froze, holding her sister. She liked him. Ah, hell. Was she experiencing the same thing Paris was? Was she falling for the person who helped her? Londyn closed her eyes, enjoying the warmth of her sister's embrace. Yet again, her mind returned to the bathroom, where she watched him shower. There wasn't any embarrassment on her part, nor on his, as she watched him wash the blood away. His body was corded with muscle and well-endowed, but he didn't get aroused. That single factor made her feel safer than anything else ever would have.

"We should probably get up," Paris suggested from where they were huddled. A hand appeared in front of Londyn's face, and she looked up. Ice, with a towel over his shoulder and a knife in his hand, offered her assistance. Those vivid blue eyes stared at her. She put her hand in his, and he lifted her off the floor. Paris got up unassisted and walked over to where Manuel was frying bacon.

"I can do this." Londyn motioned to the stove.

"Go sit down. Better yet, get a bottle of wine out of that fridge." Ice pointed to the wine cooler.

Londyn looked from it to him. "I wouldn't take you for a wine drinker."

"No?" He looked up and winked at her. *Winked.* "If it pairs well with my meal, I'm all about wine."

Londyn had no idea what to say about that. She limped over to the cooler. Her hip hurt from where she'd fallen before Bruce had dragged her to the study. She selected a crisp Pinot Noir and opened it. "Paris, help me with the table, please."

Together, they had the place settings on the table as Manuel and Ice filled each plate with food. Ice sat down last, facing Manuel.

Manuel bowed his head, as did Paris. Londyn blinked as they prayed together. She turned her wide-eyed gaze toward Ice. He watched with obvious disinterest until they were done.

"Religious?" Ice asked before he shoveled a forkful of scrambled eggs into his mouth.

"I am. I was hired to work in private security. Not a prison guard. I asked forgiveness every night."

"And yet you said you'd kill the men to get the women off the island." Ice lifted an eyebrow.

"One does extraordinary things in extraordinary situations." Manuel shrugged. "It isn't something I take lightly, and it would torment me for the rest of my life, but I would do what was needed to protect Paris and her sister."

Londyn took a bite of the eggs and looked down at her plate while Manuel answered Ice. There was sautéed onion, cilantro, sweet red peppers, and something tangy …

She took another bite and savored the flavor of someone else's cooking. What was the ingredient … "Yogurt?" she asked.

"Sour cream," Ice replied. "We need to talk about sleeping arrangements."

Londyn blinked. "Paris will sleep with me."

"No, I'll stay with Manuel."

Londyn stopped with a forkful of eggs halfway to her mouth. "Excuse me?"

Paris blushed, and Manuel placed his arm around her. "She's expecting my child."

"How?" Londyn shook her head. "You were a prisoner. How …" Her eyes widened, and her fork clattered to the plate. She pointed to Manuel as she spoke to Paris. "He didn't force you, did he?"

"No!" both Manuel and Paris shouted at the same time.

"Then, how?" Londyn spread her arms.

"He watched me when the others were sleeping. When they did, he'd come in." Paris looked up lovingly at the man beside her. "It started with us just being company for each other. He covered the camera with a black patch of cloth. We had our privacy, and we had each other."

"You're so young." Londyn shook her head.

"I'm twenty. An adult."

"Barely." Londyn ran her hands over her hair and tightened her ponytail. It was a habit when she was stressed. "I don't know what to say."

"Honestly, whatever you say is a moot point." Ice took a bite of his toast. "Your food's getting cold."

Londyn's head snapped up, and she shot him a look. "Excuse me?"

He pointed at Paris. "Adult. Pregnant. Father." He pointed to Manuel when he said *Father*. He looked at her. "Sister and aunt. Suck it up. Not the best way to find out, but you know now. Get on board and get over yourself."

She snorted. "Just like that?"

Ice shrugged. "You can fight it, make a big deal about it, and hurt people's feelings, or face the facts and accept what you can't change. Stress isn't her friend right now. Both of you need to find a new normal." Ice abruptly stood. "Anyone want seconds?"

Londyn looked at her food.

"Yes, please," Paris said. Manuel took her plate and walked over to the stove. Ice never once had his back to anyone in the room.

"Please be happy for us," Paris said from across the table. "I didn't know how to tell you."

"You're just a baby yourself." Londyn felt tears welling again. Damn it. She hated tearing up.

"I'm an adult. You raised me to be a good judge of people. Manuel is a decent, God-fearing man. His family lives in the Aysén Region of Chile."

"Chile?" Londyn looked around. "That's a long way to come for a job."

Paris cocked her head. "Where do you think we are?"

A sense of panic ran up her spine. "He told me we were near Africa in the southern hemisphere." They knew who "he" was, and Londyn wouldn't mention his name.

"You're on a private island off the coast of Chile," Manuel said as he returned the plate to Paris.

"Chile?" Londyn wrapped her arms around herself. "South America." She shouldn't be surprised that she wasn't where he said they were. She had no interaction with the guards, so she hadn't heard any accents. Not that Manuel had much of one; it was very subtle. Yet again, she felt violated.

"You should eat." Ice nudged her. She blinked and glanced at her sister, who was talking with Manuel.

"I'm not hungry." She pushed the food away from her.

Ice folded bacon into his toast and took a bite, staring at her as he chewed.

Londyn felt uncomfortable under his intense concentration. "What?"

"Trying to figure you out." He took another bite of the bacon sandwich. There was only one bite left.

"Why?"

Ice shrugged and nodded to her sister, who was whispering to her child's father. "Her, she's an open book. She's in love with him. She still has a childlike innocence that this shit hasn't stripped away. Maybe that's her protective coping mechanism at work. He's still a concern. His religion is at odds with what he *said* he would do. I'm not sure I'll ever trust him. You? You've been through hell. You act like you want to be her mother. She has someone now and doesn't need you to do that. You also need someone to take care of you."

Londyn closed her eyes. "I don't need anyone." She didn't. She'd been the adult in the family since she was eighteen and Londyn was eight.

"Yes, you do. This, what's happened to you, won't be easy to deal with. Her leaving you to start her own family will be hard, too. Especially given the way you mother her."

"I am her mother. I have been since she was eight and I was eighteen." Londyn lowered her voice to a hiss as she spoke. Paris and Manuel didn't look in their direction. They were lost in their own little world. She leaned forward and grasped her plate. "Who gave you the right to psychoanalyze anyone?"

"Ah, my degree in psychiatry?"

Londyn stopped and stared at him. "You aren't that old."

"How old do I have to be?"

"At least thirty-five."

Ice chuckled. "Try thirty-eight."

She stared at his face. No wrinkles, no scars. The bluest of blue eyes, blond, almost white hair. "I don't believe it. Where did you get your degree?"

"Which one?" Ice countered and popped the rest of his sandwich into his mouth. Then, he stood to take his dishes back to the counter.

"You have more than one?"

"Associate, Bachelor, Masters, MD, and Board certified in Psychiatry. Each degree obtained at a different institution."

Londyn followed him to the sink, noticing he didn't turn his back on Manuel. "Do you really think he's dangerous?"

"He's an unknown. Therefore, he poses a risk to you and her, even though she'll never see it."

"If he hurts her ..." Londyn grasped the counter. "I couldn't..." She sniffed back tears. "Damn it, why am I crying?"

"The tears are an emotional response to not only today but the last year. You've had a hundred or so pressure caps removed in the last couple of hours, and you'll be mixed up for a while." Ice glanced over at the table. "Yo, Manuel, if you two are done eating, bring that shit over here."

Londyn moved to the side and stared at Ice, trying to categorize what she knew about him. He killed without hesitation, worked for the government, and was a doctor. The man was a huge question mark, yet she trusted him completely. *Why?* After a year of abuse, *why* did she find it so easy to trust him?

CHAPTER 6

*I*ce sighed as he locked the door behind Manuel. Paris had thrown a hissy fit. No other words for the shrieking that went on would describe it as eloquently. If Londyn hadn't been there to calm her sister down, Ice's saner self may have abandoned station and let his other side come out to play. One, or should he say, two of the many reasons he no longer practiced.

Paris and Londyn were in Londyn's room, and unless Londyn told Paris about the locks, there wasn't anything the woman could do until morning. The bathroom wouldn't be a pleasant place to spend the night, but at least Ice knew he was secure. Hell, he'd slept in a tree for over a month.

The guy could rough it. *Rough it*. Running water and electricity. Yeah, that was roughing it.

Ice went out the front door and headed back to the guardhouse. He dragged the dead men around the rock outcropping to the water's edge. Eleven trips, countless cuss words, and a few stops to rest later, Ice made his way into the house and down to the armory. He used the keys he'd taken off one of the men at the beach and found the one that opened the door. Flicking on the light, he took stock of the small but adequate armory. M4s, ammo, handguns, tasers, and a whole damn pile of zip ties. He almost missed the explosives stored under a burlap cover. C4, blasting caps, det cord, wireless detonators, the whole nine yards. That could put a hurt on someone. The weapons were coming with him because he didn't trust Manuel as far as he could throw him.

Ice had a nice little platform built up in a tree where he could store them. Five trips, zero cuss words, and a ripped knee in the borrowed jeans later, he'd tucked all the ammo and weapons into the tree. He locked the door to the armory and glanced at the camera. Well, now, wasn't that an idea? He'd have whatever computer geek showed up turn that camera on and send it to his phone.

That way, he could keep tabs on lover boy. The radio he found on the same guy with the keys was tucked away in Bruce ol' boy's room. In the off position with the battery pitched into the ocean. Not that he didn't trust what Manuel told him. Ice snorted and rolled his shoulders.

He went back into the kitchen and washed before he fixed a sandwich. Taking it outside, he moved to the garden's center and sat under the tree. God, the food was much better than the prepackaged crap he'd been existing on.

He saw the activity in Londyn's bedroom. The door opened and then shut. He waited for whoever had left to appear in the hall. Ice stopped chewing and watched, hoping it was Londyn rather than her sister. He blinked and started chewing again. Why? He looked down at his sandwich as if it had offended him. There was that feeling of being wrapped a bit around a finger again. He took another bite and looked back at the house. Because he liked that feeling. That was why he wanted it to be Londyn. As if his thoughts summoned her, Londyn moved into the kitchen and foraged around in the fridge. Then, she walked out of the kitchen and straight toward him with a water and an apple.

Sitting beside him, she handed him the water and bit into the apple. "I saw you come out here with half a loaf of French bread."

Ice took the water and looked at the sandwich he'd been eating. Fair enough, it was probably half the loaf. "Why aren't you asleep?"

"I kept seeing him die," she said and sighed. "I'm happy he's gone. No part of me cares how he died, but I can't stop picturing it."

"Have you ever seen someone killed before?" He took another bite of his sandwich.

She was silent for a long time. "Our parents. My dad killed my mom before he killed himself. They'd been divorced for years. He hated her for removing him from our lives. He loved us, but he wasn't a good dad. Couldn't keep a job. Liked his beer too much. Finally, Mom had enough."

"You were there when it happened?"

"Yeah. I made Paris stay in the bathroom and ran downstairs when I heard the yelling. I walked in just as he shot her in the head. He turned and looked at me, told me he was sorry, and then shot himself."

Fuck, she had been through hell. Ice chewed on his sandwich and took a drink of water. "Lots to unpack there."

Londyn took a bite of her apple and spoke around a mouthful of food. "I don't want to unpack it. I went through counseling. I'm over that."

When Ice turned to look at her, she glanced at him. "I'm as over it as I can get, and I don't want to talk about it." That was a better response and one he'd accept. "What organization do you work for? I can't remember if anyone ever said."

"Guardian."

She nodded. "And you want us to stay here on this island until you can get whatever information is on those computers off them."

"Or until the new guards arrive, yes."

"Why not just kill them, too?" Londyn sighed and spun the apple between her fingers.

"Mighty cavalier attitude about killing, isn't it?" Ice wasn't one to talk, but he didn't seek out reasons to kill people. He did his job.

"You killed them all. The amount of blood on you and your clothes tonight told the story." She sighed again.

"I did." He wouldn't lie. He'd killed them under orders. "It wasn't my decision, but it was the right one. Your sister needed to be removed from that situation, and if someone had figured out what had gone on here ..."

"I'll never stop hating that man," she said quietly, although the emotion behind it was intense.

"What did you do on social media?" Ice asked, redirecting her thoughts.

"I had a cooking and lifestyle channel. Those eggs were good tonight." Londyn took the bait and moved on.

"I love food."

"I can tell." Londyn nodded to his almost-gone sandwich.

Ice stared at her for a long while. The bruising on her face was noticeable, but he could imagine her on video. She was beautiful. His glance landed on her lips. He blinked and took another bite of his sandwich. Why had he noticed her lips? Why had he thought she was beautiful? Hell, he hadn't thought of anyone's looks like that in ... well, since the surgery. What in the hell had they been talking about? Oh, right. "Thirty days of dehydrated food and protein bars."

"Eww." Londyn shivered. "Nasty."

"Right? I admit I eat a lot, but my metabolism is high." He shrugged. That and he worked his ass off on the knife range, and he worked out religiously to keep fast, limber, and silent.

"How long have you worked for Guardian?" She tossed the apple core into the bushes across from them.

"A while." He wouldn't give out any information. He couldn't.

"As a ... what do they call you, a fixer? I saw that on a television show once."

"No. I don't fix things." He broke the hell out of them.

"Then what do they call what you do?"

"My job." He turned to her. "Why do you want to know?"

She sighed and leaned back against the bark of the tree. "You showed up here, killed him, and then killed eleven other men. You're keeping us here. Why not just helicopter us out of here and do what you need to do?"

"Good question." If he had to guess—and it wasn't in his job description to second-guess his superiors—it was probably a matter of surveillance. The airspace could be monitored. People landed there. People left there, so the thought would be that Brucey-boy worked with someone. Were they watching? Were his systems monitored? Was he supposed to make contact? Would failure to do so send people into a panic? Having a helicopter land and take off may send the bugs into the woodwork. "Whatever Guardian is looking for, I can guarantee that more than our organization has a vested interest in what's on this island. Your island."

"I want to go home." She wrapped her arms around her legs. "And then again, I don't. I don't want to go back to that life. I can't. Not anymore. He took that from me."

Ice popped the last bite of the sandwich into his mouth. Finally full for the first time in over a month. He finished chewing before he spoke. "If you're married to that fucker, you have enough money to do whatever you want, or nothing at all, for that matter." He shrugged. The woman had a private island that cost at least fifteen million, or that would be his guess.

"I don't want his money," she spat into the dark.

"Ha, why the fuck not? He stole a year of your life. He stole a year of your sister's. Use that money to get yourself some high-class therapy and then put it to work doing shit that would drive Brucey-boy insane." Ice drank the rest of the water.

Londyn turned to look at him. "That would be justice, wouldn't it?"

"Damn straight." Ice grinned at her. "You should try to sleep."

Londyn sighed and shook her head. "I'm sure I'll sleep sooner or later. Right now, I'm afraid to go to sleep."

"Why?"

"In case this isn't real. In case this is a nightmare, and I'm still with him or unconscious."

Ice reached over and pinched her leg.

"Ouch! Hey, what the heck?"

"Not a dream. If you were unconscious, you couldn't feel it either."

"Do you think you could just tell me that next time?" She rubbed her thigh.

"Where's the fun in that?" Ice chuckled.

Londyn shook her head. "You are really messed up, you know that, right?"

"Oh, darling, I'm so messed up. Not even my agency knows what to do with me half the time." He chuckled again.

"But you're safe," Londyn whispered.

He turned to look at her. The light evening wind blew her dark brown hair, and the gold of the moonlight kissed her skin. She looked ethereal, exhausted, and utterly defeated. "I'm safe for you and Paris, but never mistake the fact that I'm lethal if I need to be."

He wouldn't let her get any further in her transference. Clinically, he recognized it in Paris. She'd fallen in love with her "hero." In Paris's case, the erotic transference had resulted in a kid. That relationship would have problems. Paris would outgrow her sense of gratitude. He hoped for everyone's sake that Londyn took the money and got the counseling they both needed.

"Why doesn't that scare me?" Londyn asked as she stared at him.

"Because you're still in shock. Not physically, but mentally. You feel disconnected from what's happening."

Londyn shook her head. "I broke down earlier."

"And you'll do it again. You'll probably run the gambit of symptoms. Anger, anxiety, jitters, or feel as if your mind is in a fog bank."

She was silent momentarily before asking, "Should you scare me?"

"Darling, you should run away from me as fast as you can and never look back." Ice, once again, didn't pull any punches.

"Why?"

He let his eyes search the heavens. "You know what I do for a living." She wasn't an idiot. Anyone with half a brain could figure it out.

"But you work for a government agency. They have controls and cross-checks, right? The people you work for don't just pick a person and then boom, pull your trigger, right?" She unfolded her arms and legs and turned to face him.

He nodded. "There are intense cross-checks."

"Monsters like Bruce. That's who you go after?"

"Much, much worse than Brucey-boy." Ice had terminated men and women who preyed on humanity without remorse or care.

Londyn stared at him for a long time. He didn't care. She was working through shit. "Then, no, Ice, I'm not afraid of you. I'll never be afraid of you because I'll never be that type of monster." She stood up and offered him a hand. "We should both get some rest."

He stood without taking her hand. "I'll stay up. I have assistance coming tomorrow."

"Did you get a call?" she asked as they walked toward the house.

"No."

"Then how do you know?"

Ice smiled and let her go into the kitchen first.

"I know how my organization works." He'd have a computer geek and, more than likely, an operative to relieve him and watch Manuel and the women before the next sunset. Hell, they could replace him altogether. That depended on how much Guardian believed the island was monitored. They'd find out tomorrow.

CHAPTER 7

"All right, get me up to speed," Jason King said as soon as he walked into the conference room.

"Con is heading to the airstrip nearest his location for pickup," Jewell said from the computer screen on the wall.

Jason glanced up at her. "Who's going with him? Ice will need some relief. There's a possibility this is a twenty-nine-day mission, and he's already been on the island by himself for over thirty days."

"Centurion." His brother Joseph cleared his throat and shifted in his chair, drawing Jason's eyes to his brother on the computer screen. "She was available and had a cover story for an extended absence."

Jason leaned back in his chair. "Has that been cleared through *all* the channels?" He wasn't the approval authority on her use. That was above his pay grade.

"Yes. Approval was given, begrudgingly," Jacob, his youngest brother, said from the other side of the table.

"All right. Give me the rundown."

Jewell started, "Centurion and Con will parachute in. She'll do a tandem jump. Con will only need his laptop. It'll be strapped to him, and he'll be strapped to her. Once we get him in to see what's going on with that set of systems, we'll know when to send in the rescue ship."

"What about surveillance?"

"That's an unknown. We assume the island and its occupant are part of the greater picture, not the sole subject."

"And that greater picture is what exactly?" Jason looked from Jewell to Joseph and ended up landing on Jacob, who leaned forward.

"We believe this is the nerve center for a coalition orchestrating events worldwide. The problem we have with proof is simply the complete *lack* of proof. You and the Council have been briefed on the results we have followed from each time Ice said Jonas went into the computer room. Those times coincide with when computers received modified transmissions leading to the resulting actions. Missing information, incorrect data, and fraudulent reports resulted in orders being given to the military that were never issued. Rogue units performing atrocities that, from what people on the ground tell us, were computer-verified orders from leaders in other districts. Only those orders were never given."

"Yet there are time stamps of the documents being modified when we dig into the program, but there's no way to trace who modified it. We have a *when* but not a *who*. Everything points to the Clean Slate program." Jewell sighed heavily. "This could be the person who stole it from the NSA."

"The computer program that was used when Dr. Whitehead was killed. Con is the perfect person to send, then," Jason recalled with a nod.

"If you say so," Joseph grumped.

Jason rolled his eyes. "Get over it."

Jacob leaned forward, totally ignoring Joseph's grump. "Yes. It's classified at the highest level. The NSA doesn't know we know about it. The only ones who know are us in this conference, Con, and the Council."

"Then the information won't get out." Jason leaned forward and took off his glasses. "Casualties on the island?"

"Twelve. Eleven guards, one primary. The island is secure until the next shift of guards is flown in from Santiago in twenty-nine days," Joseph filled him in.

"You've confirmed this?" Jason looked at his brother Joseph. "Wasn't there something about a guard helping her sister?"

"No need to confirm. It's Ice. Eleven or twelve are down. Eleven if the information given to the woman he found at the house was true, and one of the guards is a friendly. Twelve if the information was planted or a lie. From the data Jewell has given us, they're very well-paid rent-a-cops. Ice would have sliced through them efficiently and expediently."

"What do we have on the sisters?"

"Londyn and Paris Chatsworth. The file is in front of you," Jewell said as her fingers flew across the keyboard.

Jason opened the computer file and read about the murder-suicide. "Any connection between them and our primary?"

"None. I don't get why this guy living on an

island on the coast of Chile decided to kidnap these two women. I found no connection between the girls and Chile. Of course, I can't find squat on this Bruce Jonas. He's scrubbed just as well as our Shadows. I have nothing, and I do mean nothing. Land deals on that island are all through shell companies, and Ethan is still tracing that never-ending story. It seems like the companies just replicate and multiply." Jewell shook her head. "They literally lived in two different hemispheres, and I'm lost on how to make a connection or find out information on Mr. Jonas."

Jason looked up at his sister; his brothers were watching her, too. "Do you think his systems will give you information?"

"God, Jace, I really hope so. I feel like a kinder-gartener against what this guy has done. Hopefully, Con will be able to get a foothold."

"I'm sure you'll figure things out, Button. I'll want updates as soon as Con hits the ground."

"You'll be the first person to know after he tells me. Zane will be that conduit. To Joseph and Jacob, too."

"Good. I want the NDAs signed and informa-tion about the women worked, wrapped, and sealed."

"Centurion has the NDAs, and she knows what needs to be done," Joseph informed his brother.

Jason nodded. "Joseph, you keep your thumb on Ice. I want to know if we need to get him off that island."

Joseph nodded. "I'll monitor it."

"Good. Archangel out." The computer screens faded to black, leaving Jason alone in the room with his brother Jacob. He leaned back and looked across the table. "Ice worries me. He's never had extended contact after a mission."

"He knows how to subvert the tests. Doc Wheeler said as much, but he's never given any indication of working off the scope."

"Of course, he knows what Wheeler wants to hear. He was trained by the best." Jason rubbed his chin. "Centurion knows he has … issues?"

"She does. She's prepared to handle things if need be." Jacob sighed. "We have to find out what that man was doing and who he was doing it for."

"Unless he was working alone," Jason mused.

"That wouldn't explain the people coming and going."

"Needs to be verified. That woman has been on that island for over a year. She could be suffering from altered reality."

"It's the middle of the night there. I can call and check on things."

"No. There's nothing we can do until Centurion and Con get there, no matter what has happened."

"Joseph will contact Ice right before they jump."

"Good. All right, on to other things. Let's bring in Tori. We need to talk about the kidnapping that happened in Italy."

"She's all over it. Hold on, let me get her."

Jason leaned back as Jacob left the conference room. Ice was a wild card, and he hoped like hell the man was as solid as everyone thought he was. He'd snapped once, but they'd taken him on anyway. He'd been a damn good asset because they'd been careful with his assignments. His normal mission had no interaction with anyone but the target or the target's guards. His fellow assassins knew to keep an eye on him. They never reported any problems. He hoped like hell Ice kept his shit together. Now was not the time for the man to go rogue. There was too much at stake.

CHAPTER 8

*I*ce watched Paris and Manuel in the kitchen. Londyn was still sleeping, but the two love birds were up and about. He'd made Manuel help him refill the ice bath Brucey-boy was taking before Paris woke up. He kept them away from the study and the computer room and watched Manuel like a hawk. There was something off about the guy. Something deep in his gut irritated him whenever he looked at the man. It was annoying as hell. Like he'd missed something.

When his phone vibrated in his pocket, Ice stepped out into the garden and backed away from the kitchen before answering. "Go."

Fury's voice grated over the connection. "Authenticate Snow."

"Frozen."

"Sitrep."

"Eleven guards dead. One is alive. I'm not sure how much longer. He's tripping my wire. The youngest sister is pregnant by him. Some kind of far-fetched plan to escape. I haven't been able to validate." He'd search every square inch of the island. If that fucking boat wasn't there, he'd get Manuel to tell the truth.

"You have inbound help."

"Good. I'm fucking tired. Who?" Probably Harbinger or Malice.

"Centurion."

Ice blinked. "I didn't think Centurion or Maximus worked with the rest of us."

"Enjoy the downtime. Centurion will keep shit level while you get some rest."

"What about a computer nerd?"

"Tandem jumping about … now."

Ice looked up. He couldn't see shit. No planes … wait. A slight contrail was visible. "I see them. Damn, a high-altitude jump."

"Get the sisters to sign the NDA. Send a picture and name of the guard."

Ice dropped his phone, hit the camera, and zoomed in on Manuel. "Done."

"What about him is tripping your wire?"

"Fuck, I wish I knew. There's something …" Ice swore. "I get a vibe from the guy."

Fury was silent for a moment. "You doing okay?"

"What?" Ice was taken aback by the question.

"You know what I mean." Fury didn't pull any punches.

"Yeah, thanks for asking. I'm peachy. Are you worried that I cut everyone's throat?"

"I'm not."

"But others are." Ice snorted. "How long do I have to prove that I'm okay?"

"You killed seven people."

"I did. A lifetime ago. Val killed how many? What about Reaper? Should we talk about you?"

"I'm not up for discussion. You are."

"No, I disagree. Why is my past always brought up and none of the others?"

"They didn't have a psychotic break with reality."

"You know the reason why that happened, and so do I. I haven't had any further issues, and I'm sick of this getting thrown in my face."

"Deal with it. It's part of working for us."

Ice looked up. He could see a faint dot of what he assumed was the parachute. "I've got to go."

"Ice."

"What?"

"I have never questioned you. I never will. The ones who do have never done what we do. They couldn't. I'm directed to do so when I ask questions, not because I'm harassing you. You're just like I was. I know you're solid."

Ice looked into the kitchen. "Thanks."

"Now, go get Centurion and that fucking nerd and get some sleep."

"That sounds like a deal." Ice hung up and headed into the kitchen. He needed to secure Manuel again so he could go out of the house and meet up with his help.

* * *

ICE FOUND his help behind the house, floating down on a direct course for the helipad. The landing was perfect, and he immediately knew who the computer nerd was. Not who he expected, but the burly man unfastened himself from the tandem harness and planted his ass on the ground.

He threw the oxygen mask off and then dropped onto his back. "What a fucking rush!"

Ice rolled his eyes and moved to the woman who'd removed her oxygen mask. "Centurion?"

"Ice?"

"Yup."

She unsnapped her harness as she spoke, but her right hand was near that automatic holstered to her thigh. "Authenticate Snow."

"Frozen. Want me to sing you the song? My niece loves it." He'd sung the song with Brooke too many times to count.

The woman relaxed and moved her hand away from her weapon. "Nah, thanks. I don't want that tune in my head all day. Call me Ronnie. It's easier to say than Centurion." The woman extended her hand. "The sitrep I received was you'd extinguished any on-island threats. We're here to get him into the system and alternate shifts, so we're both ready to respond if anything happens."

"One threat remains. Maybe."

Ronnie took off her helmet, and a flood of dark brown hair fell to her shoulders. "Explain that."

Ice filled her in on Manuel and his relationship with Paris. "My gut tells me something's off."

"I'll keep a close eye on him. Con, are you going to live?"

The man looked over at them. His helmet was still on and cranked sideways, but the smile on his face was pure adrenaline rush. "Ronnie, that shit was awesome. I have to do that again." Con sat up and looked at Ice. "Take me to your computers."

"Right this way." Ice waited as they gathered their equipment. Then they walked across the island and around the massive compound. "The door to the computer area is biometric. I used the dead man to open it, then put him on ice because I didn't know if any of the computers would require the same scans."

"Smart. How many stations are there?" Con asked as they walked.

Ice snorted. "Not my specialty, and I didn't stick around to count. I made sure there was no threat and left the rest for you. The main door is propped open. I knew there wasn't anyone else in the house. There won't be any surprises. I figured you'd have the thrill of finding out what was in that place."

"A big area?" Ronnie asked.

"Massive room. Blocks transmissions and such. But now that he's here, it isn't my concern."

"True that," Con said as they walked into the house. Londyn was waiting for them.

"Londyn, this is Ronnie. She's going to help me, and this is Con. He's going to work on the computer systems."

"I'd say welcome, but under the circumstances." Londyn let the greeting drop.

"I'll take them to the computer room and then let Manuel out."

Londyn's head whipped around, her eyes wide. "He's not here. Neither is Paris. I thought they were with you?"

"Shit. Ronnie, with me." Ice pointed at Con. "There are weapons in the canopy of the tree. Londyn knows which one. Get one and protect her."

He sprinted after Ronnie, who shouted back, "Where would they go?"

"The fucker said he had a ship's captain bringing a skiff to the island. The only place to launch out would be this way." They ran in tandem. Ronnie had long legs and kept up. Ice pointed. "Go around that way. I'll come in from the front. He won't know you're here."

"On it." Ronnie diverted and hauled ass.

Ice rushed through the underbrush and crashed into the small cove. Manuel whipped around, a knife in one hand, Paris gripped with the other. "Stop, or I'll kill her!" Manuel pulled Paris closer and lined the knife up with her neck. Tears ran down Paris's face.

Ice walked forward slowly. "You don't want to do that. I'll kill you if you do." He continued to walk toward the couple.

"Stop!" Manuel jerked the knife closer to Paris's throat. A thin trail of red dripped down the column of her neck.

Ice stopped and lifted his hands out to his sides. "Why?" He didn't give a flying fuck, but he needed to give Ronnie time to set up. He needed to maneuver Manuel a bit if she set up where he thought she would. He casually sidestepped, causing Manuel to move. "What are you going to gain by taking her?"

"Money," Manuel sneered. "You said it yourself. Her sister's rich. Do you know what it's like to have nothing?"

Ice nodded. "I do." He'd lost everything when he'd had his breakdown. He would never allow that to happen again. "But hurting her has sealed your fate."

"Manny, why?" Paris sobbed. "You said you loved me. Our baby ..."

"Shut up." The man jerked her back against him. "Stupid and gullible. Do you think they would have let me into your room? No, there were several involved. I pulled the short end of the stick and fucked you. The boss would have paid for her return. He wouldn't have hesitated. You fucked everything up. Millions, he would have paid millions!" Paris collapsed in tears. Manuel backed toward the water. "I'm taking her. Her sister will pay. You come any closer, and I'll hurt her more."

Ice shook his head. "No, you won't." He looked toward the rocky abutment and nodded.

Manuel's head exploded before Ice could turn his head back, and then the body fell forward on top of Paris. The woman screamed and pushed at the dead weight on top of her.

Ice tossed the man off her and lifted her into his arms. "You're safe now." Paris clung to him. Her body was racked with sobs that shook him as he held her.

Ronnie slid down the rock face and landed in the sand at the bottom. She trotted over and glanced down at the man. "Shark bait?"

"Yes." Ice adjusted Paris's slight weight in his arms. "I'll meet you back at the compound."

Ronnie didn't waste any words as she grabbed Manuel's feet and dragged him toward the surf.

Paris was inconsolable, which was to be expected. The woman was used as a ploy. Fucking small-minded people who had no idea the hell Brucey-boy would have rained down on them. A few of the man's keystrokes apparently wiped out villages or started civil wars. A couple of small-time kidnappers holding something valuable to him for ransom would have been nothing for the man to stop. Fucking ignorant people with delusions of grandeur.

Londyn was at the front door, and Con had a gun leveled at him, safety off and loaded. *Well, kudos to the nerd.*

Ice walked straight to Londyn's bedroom and placed Paris on the bed. Londyn covered her with a blanket before she pulled him away. "What happened?"

"The game plan always was to kidnap her and make Brucey-boy pay to get her back. Manuel said some of the others were involved."

"Oh, God." Londyn pulled her hands through

her hair. "What do I do? How can I make this better?"

"You can't. She needs to process this. Stay with her. Don't ask questions. Just be there for her, and for God's sake, don't tell her everything will be okay. For her, it won't be. Not for some time. Tell her you're here for her. Tell her you'll get her help."

Londyn nodded. "Thank you." She turned and went over to the bed, crawling onto the other side and wrapping Paris in her arms.

Ice let the sisters deal with the latest mound of shit they had to work through and returned to Con.

The man was in the computer room. The weapon in his hand was still on fire and still loaded. "Do you know how to use that thing?"

Con looked down at the weapon in his hand. "You pull the fucking trigger, right?"

Ice chuffed out a laugh. "Right."

Con lifted the weapon, keeping the muzzle pointed away from anything that would be damaged, dropped the magazine, rode the slide to the rear, caught the bullet loaded in the chamber, rode the slide forward, and slid the selector to safe. He thumbed the round into the magazine and placed the weapon on a small shelf by the door. All actions were deftly completed. The man knew his way around weapons, which was good to know.

"This place is more than I expected." Con turned and walked to the first dome. "No biometrics on this computer. Hold on. I'll check the rest. We can get rid of the guy in the bathtub if they're all the same."

Ice glanced back when Ronnie walked into Bruce's office. "Taken care of. The skiff would have made the coast on a calm day. Any storm would have scuttled it. What was his story?"

"Blackmail. He and some others probably gained Paris's trust, so she wouldn't freak out and fight them when they made a run for it."

"So, they were just going to leave the other sister?"

Ice nodded. He'd been thinking about that, too. "The note slipped to Londyn told her to do what she needed to do, that Paris would be safe. If Bruce beat Londyn to death, Paris's return would have been much more important to the man." The words he'd overheard before he killed the two men on the beach made more sense now.

"I have documents those women need to sign." Ronnie pulled a leather pouch out of the small pack she had on her back.

"Now's not a good time." Ice shook his head.

Ronnie looked at him. "Now is the only time." She walked out of the room with the documents in her hand.

Ice ground his teeth together. Ronnie was right, of course, but damn it, they'd been through a fuckton of shit and needed a break.

"Ah, Iceman, dude, you need to come see this shit," Con called him from the depths of the room.

Iceman? Whatever. Ice rolled his shoulders. What type of techno shit could possibly interest him. "Where are you?"

"All the way in the back. Not a dome, a room." Con's voice pulled him farther into the massive room. He wound his way through the domes and found the door Con was talking about. He walked in and blinked before turning and taking in what he saw. Every surface of the walls and some of the ceiling held pictures of Londyn. There were screens with what must have been her channel playing and … the sick fucker. Nude shots of Londyn in the shower and while she was dressing … a shot of her strapped down in a chair, and a bloody tooth held in a plier. *The fucker.*

"There's more." Con pointed toward a door. Ice

walked in and shook his head in disgust before quickly stepping out. He shut the door behind him.

"Sick fuck," Con said. "Not my expertise, but it seems that guy had a fixation on Londyn."

"It is my expertise, and I'd say you called it correctly." Ice looked around the room again.

"I've never seen a sex doll before. I thought those were internet jokes," Con said as he headed to the door.

"Obviously not." The one in the small room with the bed had been used. The evidence was all over the plastic. The smell was enough to make him gag.

"Okay, well, getting this shit out of my brain and moving on. We have fifteen domes. None have biometrics, so you can feed that bastard to the crabs. As long as that main door stays open, he's not needed."

"I'll take the fucker off the hinges." Ice needed to destroy something while the images of that room processed. "Can you get into these machines?"

"Don't know. Just looking right now, but I've got to call in and let them know what I'm working with. Before I do that, I'm going to sit down and see what that bastard was working with." Con went to the first dome inside the door. "Do you need anything from me before I bury myself in code?"

"Nope." Ice examined the hinges. He didn't need tools. He slipped his Ka-Bar out of its sheath and used the tang under the bolt of the hinge. He popped the bottom of the knife with his fist, and the bolt moved up. Ice repeated the process on all three bolts. Ronnie walked back in as he was ready to remove all the bolts. "Shove something under the door, will you?"

She looked at what he was doing and then walked over to Bruce's desk. She foraged through drawers and returned with two small books, which she slid under the door, using her foot to push underneath the heavy weight of the metal doors. "I'll hold it steady. Pop those suckers."

Ice went to work. Together, they held the metal door after it was released from the hinges. "Fuck, I didn't think this through," Ronnie groaned. "Con, come here."

The guy leaned back in his chair and looked at them. "Oh, shit." He scrambled from his chair and grabbed the side of the door Ronnie was gripping. "On the count of three, we'll control the tip and hopefully lean it toward the wall." Con squatted and gripped the bottom of the door; Ice grabbed the upper portion.

"Three," Ice said, and the men maneuvered what felt like a two-ton door to the wall. Ice dropped his back to the wall beside the door. "Thanks."

"No worries. All that gym time was finally used." Con rolled his shoulders and headed back to the computer terminal where he was working.

"I'm checking in," Ronnie said from the desk. She palmed her phone and hit a button. "Operator Two Seven Four, standby Sunset Operative twenty."

"Man, it's good to hear her voice again," Ronnie said quietly.

"That's the truth," Ice agreed. Guardian was back in action. It didn't have the same structure, but the support, mission, and oversight were the same, and the familiarity of it was comforting.

"Authenticate Roman." Fury's voice ripped through the connection.

"Caesar," Ronnie authenticated.

"Status?"

"NDAs signed. Con is assessing the hardware. All threats eliminated." She rattled off the status.

"All threats? What happened to lover boy?" Fury asked.

"I blew his brains out when he tried to kidnap the younger sister." Ronnie sounded bored, as if the incident was nothing. Her attitude lifted her a couple of rungs on his respect ladder.

"Where the fuck was Ice?"

Ice dropped his head back and drawled, "I was there distracting him so she could take the shot." He was tired and needed a couple of hours of sleep.

"Explain the situation with the baby daddy," Fury demanded.

Ice sat down on the desk. "Best I can tell, it was lucky for Paris and unlucky for the guards. I thwarted a couple of the guards kidnapping Paris and holding her for ransom the night you told me to remove the target. Stupid fuckers thought it was easy money and the target would pay the ransom." Ice yawned hard enough to crack his jaw.

"They had no idea who they were working for," Fury added almost to himself.

"Do *we* know who the hell he is?" Ronnie asked.

"I don't care." Ice yawned again. "Do you need anything else from me? If not, I'm going to turn Brucey-boy into crab fodder and then hit the hay."

"Get some sleep. I'll contact Ronnie if I need anything else. Con will connect with CCS, so you two are on an island retreat until we can get that information. Don't get fat and lazy."

"Lazy?" Ice lifted an eyebrow.

"I'm more offended at the fat comment," Ronnie huffed.

"Well, now that you're both insulted, my work is done. The Rose is out."

Ronnie dropped her head. "He'll never change."

"How long have you known him?" Ice asked as he stood up. He didn't really care, but he was getting chatty, probably due to the lack of sleep. That shit needed to stop.

"I've known him most of my life." The woman leaned back in the chair. "Do you need help with your target?"

"Oh, hell no." Ice snorted. "I'm going to make mincemeat out of the fucker and feed the crabs."

"Rather violent." Ronnie stared at him.

"If you saw what that fucker did to Londyn, you'd be out there helping me dice him up." Ice stretched.

"Probably. Glad I didn't. I've got this. I'll see you when you wake up."

"That could be tomorrow or the next day," Ice

said as he walked back to the bathtub, where his target was getting soggy.

"Don't care. There are no threats, and we'll keep it that way," Ronnie called after him.

He stood in front of the tub and stared at the man who'd done so much damage to Londyn, Paris, and the world. Having a crab pick his bones was a fitting ending for the piece of shit.

CHAPTER 9

*C*on glanced at the evening sky and waited for Jewell to pick up.

The connection clicked, and Jewell spoke rapidly. "Hey, sorry, I was out with Dude. We were getting ready to head to bed. What do you have?"

"A hell of a mess." He glanced up at the sky. "It'll take a hot minute to break into his systems. I don't know what code he converted the crypto into, but I don't recognize it."

"Damn, smart cookie, huh?"

"Damn smart. Raspberry smart." Con knew Jewell would understand the reference. The aforementioned company used a computer chip designed for mobile phones, and eighty percent of the graphics processor on that chip was custom code. Only twenty percent was visible as the ARM processor. Still, dedicated hackers broke the code by reconstructing the language even though they didn't know how the processing worked.

"Shit. How much code do we have to work with?"

"If I had to guess, maybe five percent." Con dropped down onto a rock and looked out into the ocean. "I could use Brando on this."

"Physically or remotely?" Jewell asked.

"There's nothing for him to do remotely, but until we get in, I can't copy the data. Oh, and our target uses fiber optics. I don't know where it was run from or where it runs to, but it's shielded."

"That's why we weren't able to find any output."

"Depending on how long and eloquent the groundwork for the fiber system is, it could end anywhere," Con agreed. "Based on what I'm seeing at this compound, money wasn't an issue, and the thought that went into this hub is as good as, if not better than, the pods we have."

"Damn." Jewell sighed. "Okay. I have to send this up the line. Get some sleep, and I'll have Brando coming to you by tomorrow morning."

"I'll need more than just him."

"I'll get you the people and resources you need,

even if I have to wage war with the Department of Energy or the Office of Science. This won't beat us. It can't."

Con closed his eyes. Jewell wouldn't be able to access those kinds of resources, but he was glad she knew the extent it would take to get shit done. "How did he drill into the systems? That's what I keep coming back to. How? I know he covered his tracks by using the NSA program, but how did he break through the firewalls of some of those organizations? Have we missed something?"

Jewell was silent for a moment. "No. Shit. That makes sense."

"What makes sense?" Con knew he was tired, but damn it, Jewell was more confusing than normal.

"A program that can drill through firewalls. That's why they were after her."

"Who's her? Who are they?" He shot off the questions.

"Honor. Look, I think this guy got a hold of a program one of our best has built. We have the code engrained into our Godzilla gateway to prevent it from happening to any of our systems, but ..."

"He'd drill through with the program, do what

he needed or was paid to do, and then back out with the stolen NSA program."

"Bingo. Corrupt files were inserted or files deleted, orders changed or countermanded, and no one knows how access was gained. He backs out with the NSA program, and boom. No tracks."

"We can prove it if I can get into this system." Con drew a deep breath. They had this fucker. It was only a matter of time—the time they didn't have. Con didn't want any further bloodshed to be on his hands, and that asshat Fury told him point blank that if he didn't get the shit off the computers in thirty days, there would be more death on the island.

"We'll get there. Give me time to rally the resources here. Get some rest. It might be a long month," Jewell said, and then, the connection was gone.

"You know it won't be on you." Con jumped at Ronnie's voice.

"What?"

"What Fury said before we boarded the plane. Nothing that happens on this island is because of you. You're doing a job. Guardian is making the calls. It isn't on you."

Con bristled at the fact that Ronnie could read

his fucking mind. "How did you know I was thinking that?"

She chuckled. "It's an inherited trait, I guess. I'm tuned into people." She sat down on the rock next to him. "So, it's going to be a rough time for you?"

"Yeah. A lot of work. Tedious, but if we can grab an Exascale computer, it would help." Con laughed. "The problem is we would have to create a product package. For that, we'd need to borrow one of the Department of Energy's computational science leaders. Once that was done, it would take the computer no time to crack the code this guy uses."

"So, ask Guardian to do that." Ronnie shrugged.

Con barked out a laugh. "Not so easy. These machines are working on large-scale, as in the entire world type of issues, and they're booked for years. Additionally, getting one of the super-geeks to help us would take an act of Congress. Those guys are priceless."

"Call Jewell and tell her what you need. You're underestimating what Guardian can do."

"She knows." Con chuckled. "She knows."

"Then, go get some sleep. It's been a long day."

"Technically, we're still in our yesterday, so

you're right. This day has lasted almost forty-eight hours."

"Geek." Ronnie nudged him.

He turned to look at the woman. She was beautiful and playful and way out of his league. "I'm not a geek. I'm uber intelligent."

"Oh, I'm sorry." She batted her eyes and put her fingers in front of her lips comically.

Con chuckled. "How did you get into this line of work?"

Ronnie's smile faded. "A family situation. Have you ever felt absolutely helpless?"

"Damn straight." Con had, and he vowed he'd never give anyone that control over him again. His talents ensured it.

"Ever want to feel that way again?"

"Nope."

"That's how I got into this line of work." Ronnie shrugged. "Never again. Never vulnerable. Never powerless."

Con nodded. "Hell of a motto."

"Damn straight. As long as it takes, right?"

"Whatever it takes." Con nodded. Guardian was full of diverse people, but everyone was the salt of the earth—good people working for a damn good organization.

* * *

"You need what?" Jason cleared his throat.

Jewell sighed and repeated herself. "I need you to contact the Department of Science or Energy and get us time on one of their Exascale computers and the use of one of their programmers."

"Why?"

"Jason, weren't you listening?" Jewell threw her hands up in the air.

"Button, I heard every word and understood every sixth you said. So, dumb it down for me, okay?"

Jewell nodded and took a deep breath. "Okay, sorry. This guy, Bruce Jonas, has what I would call a super pod going on. Think of the work we did on these pods and then add what I believe is an elaborate mesh of fiber optics that could, in theory, route his transmissions anywhere in the world before he accessed the systems he wanted. Impossible for us to track unless he made a mistake and say ... found the woman he was obsessing about and married her online. Following?"

"I am." Jason nodded.

"Okay, then we're adding an encryption issue. Think of it as trying to read a book in a language you don't understand, and you only have a correlation for two letters from your language to this new one. Then, add that you don't know if your alphabet and this foreign language have the same length or if there are added symbols that don't correlate with anything you've heard or seen before."

"That's what Con is up against?" Jason asked.

"Yes." Jewell did a mental fist pump. Zane patted her hand. He knew how hard it was for her to explain things sometimes. "Now, for another layer of frosting on this cake … I think Bruce Jonas was using Honor's code that drilled through firewalls and then the NSA's cloaking program to erase his presence in the systems."

"I knew about the cloaking program. That's what we briefed the Council to get their agreement to take out Bruce."

"But if he were using Honor's program, it would explain why someone was after her."

Jason nodded as Jewell watched him on the screen. He stopped and cocked his head. "Why would he use her program and not develop one of his own?"

"Time, lack of desire, why re-create the wheel? Take your pick. From the information we're getting from Ice, Con, and Ronnie, this guy was amusing himself with women and was doing the computer thing a few hours a day at most." She had no idea what mental issues Bruce had besides agoraphobia, but being sadistic and a killer totes needed to be added to the stack.

"Let me see what I can do." Jason took off his glasses and rubbed his eyes. "Send me a point of contact in both agencies, please."

"They're in your inbox. This is important, Jace. If we can get that data, we might be able to find out who was ordering or funding the stuff he was doing." Jewell about vibrated off her chair. They were being put to the test, and it was one she couldn't fail.

"That I understand, Button. I'll do what I can. Anything else?"

Jewell cocked her head. "Isn't that enough?"

Jason laughed. "Yes. Yes, it is. Goodnight."

"Night." Jewell disconnected the video and spun toward Zane. "I'm worried."

"Why?"

"I'm afraid of what this will lead to. I've got a bad feeling." She pulled a pencil out of her hair and bit at the metal where the eraser used to be.

Zane pulled the pencil from her mouth. "That

feeling is something we trust, but we can't act on it except to accept it's there." He extended his hand and stood up. She stood, too, and leaned into him. "What would I ever do without you?"

"Work yourself into a grave." Zane chuckled. "That's something I'm not willing to let happen. I love you."

"I love you, too." She toed up to kiss him, but Dude nosed in between them.

"My man, you've got to learn some manners." Zane moved the dog after patting him on the head. "Now, where were we?" He pulled her into his arms, and Jewell let herself melt into the man who was her sanity, rock, and soul mate.

CHAPTER 10

*L*ondyn held her sister in the darkness of her room. She stared at the camera that was always illuminated. The absence of the flashing light seemed surreal.

"What was it like for you?" Paris asked.

Londyn sighed. "It was bad sometimes. Most of the time, it was … He watched me all the time. For some reason, he needed me to submit to him and tell him I wanted him. I wouldn't do it. After a couple of months, I started pushing him."

"Pushing him?" Paris adjusted her pillow.

"Pushing his limits, you know. I hated that he controlled everything I did."

"No, not you," Paris deadpanned, and they both laughed a little. Londyn was a control freak. Which was another reason she hated him monitoring her every move.

"Yeah, who would have thought it?" Her smile faded. "What about you?"

Paris closed her eyes. "I was so scared and lonely. I craved any kind of personal contact. The first time he talked to me. I cried. He asked what my name was. I cried. No one had talked to me. No one answered my questions. I had some books, and that was it. They brought me food and cleaning supplies in these small bottles. Nothing sharp."

"Oh, God, had you thought about ..."

"It crossed my mind, but I couldn't. The fear of not knowing what was happening or why ... If it weren't for those books, I'd be insane."

"I'm so sorry."

Paris shook her head. "It wasn't your fault. That's on him. On them. I thought he loved me. I thought he cared. He seemed so genuine."

"Did you love him?" Londyn pushed a lock of hair back so she could see her sister.

"I don't know ... Yes, I thought I did. I thought he loved me, too. Oh, God, how can I miss him and want him to be alive? He was using me."

"You didn't know that. How could you have prevented falling in love with him when they planned it so you had no choice? He didn't want you to know. *They* didn't want you to know."

Paris wiped at a tear that flowed from her eye to the bridge of her nose. "I'm pregnant."

The statement stood on its own, didn't it? Besides the trauma of being held captive in relative solitude for almost a year, her sister had a bigger issue to deal with. "Do you know how far along?" Londyn rolled over and grabbed another tissue for her sister.

"I haven't had my period in two months. We made love about a week before he left last time. I didn't have it after he left or the following month when he wasn't here. The thing is, I really wanted this baby. I wanted it so bad." Paris sniffled and wiped at the tears.

"Wanted?" Londyn couldn't imagine the pain Manuel's treachery caused Paris.

"Want. She didn't do anything to anyone. It isn't her fault either."

"She?" Londyn smiled.

Paris's sad smile warmed a bit. "Yeah, it's just a feeling."

"It won't be easy, but I'll be there for you and her."

Paris lowered her eyes. "I can't go back to our

lives the way they were before. I'm not that person anymore. I had so much time to think, to worry, to plan. I don't want to go back to school—all those people. I think I'd crawl into a corner and cry. I'm terrified that somehow this reprieve will be taken away from us."

"No, we're safe. I trust Ice. I trust him with our lives." Londyn was certain he'd protect them. She knew it within the depths of her soul. He was dangerous, that was true, but he'd never become a danger to them. He was their protector, and having seen what the man could do, she knew they were secure in ways they'd never been before. Ice was a predator, but they weren't his prey. He was focused on defending them. Londyn sighed. She trusted the man with her life. Literally. There was no room for any doubt. The feeling resonated throughout her body.

"Why?"

"He's honest, and he doesn't pull any punches. If I didn't know better, I'd think he was on the spectrum."

"So, he's autistic?" Paris's brow creased.

Londyn chuffed out a small laugh. "No, I don't think he is. It's just that his mannerisms are reminiscent of Larry, you know?"

"Larry. I haven't thought of him in a long time. I wonder if he's doing okay."

Londyn made a sound of agreement before adding, "I've wondered that, too. He was a good neighbor."

"He was, and I'm sure he's fine. Nobody messed with him. He was so big, nobody would."

"All that time to lift at the gym where he worked," Londyn added.

Paris sighed. "I don't have a job, and I'm going to have a baby. How in the hell is that going to work?"

"I don't know, but we'll figure it out."

"Not we, Londyn, *me*. I'm going to be a mom, and I need to be able to figure this out."

Londyn stopped and drew a breath. "I can understand you wanting to do this by yourself, but you don't need to."

Paris wiped at the tears that still came even though she'd cried almost all day and night. Her eyes were puffy and red, but she'd never looked better to Londyn. She was safe, and they would leave the island sooner or later. Hopefully sooner.

"I'm so scared all the time. I just can't shake the feeling." Paris shivered next to her.

"Right now, there's nothing to be afraid of. Ice,

135

Ronnie, and Con are here. Ice is an army by himself. He has two people helping him now. We're safe."

"If we stay here, but what happens when we leave?" Paris asked and closed her eyes.

"Just rest. We can worry about tomorrow, tomorrow. We're safe right now, and that's all that matters." She closed her eyes and hoped she could take her own advice. What was going to happen when they left the island? Where would they go? How would they support themselves? Where could they raise a baby? She rolled onto her back and stared at the dark corner of the room. That bastard had stripped every sense of security they had away from them. Damn him. She hoped he was burning in hell.

CHAPTER 11

"*H*ey, Doc." Ice rubbed his face. He'd slept like the dead. Brucey-boy's bed was damn comfortable, but he needed to relieve Ronnie after making a few phone calls.

Jeremiah Wheeler chuckled. "Hey, right back at you, Doc. Are you doing all right?"

"Me? Yeah, no worries. I'm calling because of my current mission. I haven't talked to management yet, but I think they'll agree."

"Did anyone ever tell you that you tend to leave a person out of most of your thoughts when you have a conversation?"

Ice snorted. "I tend to do that when I know the answers."

"Well, how about you fill in the blanks for those of us in the cheap seats?"

"My current mission has a couple of women who have been mentally and physically abused. Long-term, over a year. They were held captive. The eldest was physically and emotionally abused. The youngest was held in solitary confinement and then was used by several guards as a golden goose. One of the guards got close, and now, she's pregnant. The baby daddy tried to kidnap her, had a knife to her throat, and drew some blood. We took him out."

"In front of her?"

"He fell on top of her," Ice confirmed.

"Shit."

"Eloquently said, Dr. Wheeler."

"Thank you. All right. I'll call management and start developing a plan to help them, assuming they want help."

"They will." He'd make damn sure of it.

"May I ask a question?"

"If I said no, would it stop you?" Ice countered.

"No."

"Well?" The sarcasm dripped from Ice's voice.

"Why are you calling me about this?"

Ice drew a deep breath. "I've asked myself that question since I woke up and about a hundred times before I dialed your number. I don't know how to explain why I needed to tell you personally. These two, they need help. They've been fucked over, Jeremiah. Fucked hard. The oldest, Londyn, she's strong, but I see the cracks forming. They're codependent, and the detritus of this situation will fuck with that dynamic, too. The youngest, she's carrying a baby from a man who was willing to ransom and ultimately kill her."

"The older sister. Tell me about her."

Ice laid back on the bed and closed his eyes. "She's fierce. Man, she stands up. She had to be strong to survive what my target put her through. She's raised her kid sister. Yeah, she stands up. Straight up."

"You like her."

"What?"

"You like her. The only people you refer to as stand-up people are your few friends."

Ice frowned. "Don't need you to psychoanalyze me, J."

"I'm not. We've talked, and I think we have at least a pseudo-relationship. That comment is just something I've noticed you say when you talk about those you trust."

"Right. Okay." Ice didn't believe it for a minute, but whatever. "I respect her." Which was a hell of an admission for him. When he was with Mal and Flack, he talked about women—women who didn't exist. Only his friends didn't know it. He'd been celibate since the break. Keeping himself on that side of reality was his main goal in life. Worrying about anyone else or anything else was damn hard to do. His friends and their families were as much as he wanted to handle.

"You know it's all right to like her, right?" Jeremiah coaxed.

"I do. And thank you, but I don't need your permission." He closed off the conversation.

"Your prognosis is excellent. That tumor isn't coming back."

"And if it does? Will I have another break? Will I have hallucinations again? The disordered thinking? Letting myself get close to anyone who doesn't know what happened could be a death sentence for them." Ice hadn't called to get into that topic again.

"That's fear talking," Jeremiah chided him.

"I don't feel that sensation any longer." He didn't. He wasn't afraid of anything. He also didn't feel anxiety. That made him damn good at what he did.

"So, you'd rather go through life alone? Your scans are clear and have been for years. The tumor won't come back." Jeremiah sighed. "You're a doctor. You know the statistics, especially after five years. You're working on seven. Give yourself a break."

"I can't." Ice closed his eyes. "I killed those people because I thought they would kill me."

"And they probably would have. That gang would have killed you for being in their territory, and you stopped a major shipment of cocaine into the country."

"But I didn't *know* that." It was just luck. Luck that the police were fixated on the amount of drugs at the scene. Luck that he collapsed before the cops could question him and luck that the emergency room doctor thought to get a brain scan because of his behavior when he was admitted. The tumor that could have killed him was removed, and the following treatment changed him in a way no one could have predicted.

So, yeah, it was also luck that Demos sought him out and gave him purpose again. A purpose and a mission he felt to his core. Loyalty was something he valued. Empathy toward other people was practically impossible, and things that used to bother him no longer did. He didn't care about people in a very general way. Forming relationships took time. It took work, and even then, the ties were loose, and he could sever them and walk away.

"One step at a time, Ice."

"Fuck you, one step at a time, J.," Ice retorted.

Jeremiah laughed. "I'll work with management to get the women help."

"Thanks."

"Hey, Ice?"

"Yeah?"

"How long will this mission last?"

"Up to thirty days," Ice responded.

"If you need me, I'm here, as always."

Ice rolled his eyes. "I'm not hearing voices. I'm not paranoid. I'm firmly rooted in the present. I want the women to get help because I witnessed some of the shit my target put them through. I don't need a date with my shrink."

"Huh. Well, I was talking about the women and being here if they need me, but ..."

Ice snorted. "Bye, Doc." He hung up and dropped the phone to his chest. His hand went to the top of his head and the scar where they'd sawed through his skull. Yeah, he was lucky. Lucky to be alive. He'd learned to mask his darkness. That was what he called the intensely intoxicating experience of not giving a shit about anything or anyone. He let himself slip into the shadows of his mind when he worked and forced himself out of the darkness to interact with humanity. It would be ridiculously easy to stay where he didn't feel, didn't care, and didn't have any desire to do so. Yet his years of training, learning about the brain and how it functioned, wouldn't allow him to stay on that side. The rational part of his mind kept him from slipping into the darkness and staying there. His friends kept him from slipping. Brooke ... he smiled. That little girl touched him in a way no one else had. He was fiercely protective of her and found himself wanting her to be happy. He pitied anyone stupid enough to mess with his honorary niece.

Did he like Londyn? Ice stared at the ceiling and watched the fan spin slowly above the bed.

Yes. He respected her strength. Further, he respected the way she thought. She wasn't afraid of him because she wasn't a monster. That was what she'd said. Ice smiled. Her logic was so similar to his.

A whiff of something delectable hit his nose. His stomach grumbled loud enough to wake the entire house. Ice tossed off the covers and strode naked into the bathroom. He took a quick shower and pulled on his own clothes that had been laundered.

Before he left the room, he ensured his knives were secured in their scabbards and attached to his body. There wasn't a known threat on the island, but he wasn't careless. He stopped, dropped into one of the massive chairs by the fireplace, and placed another call.

"Operator Two Seven Four. Standby, Sunset Operative Sixteen."

Ice drew another deep breath. Bacon and cinnamon. Damn, it smelled fantastic.

"Authenticate Snow."

"Frozen," Ice replied. "I've been out for the last eight hours. What's the sitrep?"

"Computer geek needs resources. Management

is working it. No new information on Jonas. Ronnie related all was good when she checked in. Aerial surveillance shows no flights over or toward the island. We're monitoring the security firm that sends out the guards. Nothing there. You're good to go."

"Roger that. So, babysit until relieved, or all hell busts loose."

"Correct," Fury responded.

"All right. I contacted Wheeler today."

"For?"

Ice smiled. Fury didn't ask if he was okay. He fucking liked that about the ancient one. "To get help for the women. I figured management wouldn't mind."

"Don't see how they could, but I'll clear it anyway. Like you should have."

"Meh, I'm an ask forgiveness instead of permission kind of guy," Ice quipped.

"Join the crowd. Anything else?"

"I'm going to do a deep search of the island today. If we can get the computer geek to get the monitors and alarms up around the place, we can sleep at night and work during the day. I'm assuming Con will need all hands on deck eventually."

"Sounds like a plan. Are you asking permission or telling me?"

"Telling you, reference my statement about not asking for permission." Ice chuffed.

"Check in tomorrow. Same time."

"Will do." Ice disconnected and stood up. He was going to follow his nose to those amazing smells.

CHAPTER 12

*L*ondyn grabbed the blueberry Dutch baby pancake from the oven and set it on the trivet. She'd slept fitfully, waking every time Paris moved. Catching movement by the door, she glanced up. Her attention slipped, and her hand hit the hot metal of the pan she'd just pulled from the oven.

"Damn," she hissed as the cast iron skillet clattered loudly against the granite countertop.

Ice was beside her instantly. "Cool water," he said as he moved her to the sink. He started the tap and held her hand under the water.

"It isn't that bad," Londyn told him and tried to pull her hand back.

"Let someone take care of you for a change." Ice turned his head and stared at her. His intense blue eyes were so close as their gazes met.

She looked down and then at her hand. "It's been a long time," she whispered under her breath.

"I believe you." Ice's voice was level and matter-of-fact. She wasn't sure why that made her feel lighter. His large hands turned hers over as he examined the burn. "I don't think it'll blister."

"Probably not. It was stupid. I'm just not used to …"

"People being around?"

"Yeah, in the mornings, he'd wait—"

"For you to bring him his breakfast in the office. Lunch, too," Ice said and turned off the water. He reached for a towel and blotted her hand dry.

"That's right. You watched."

"Real men don't treat people like he did. You have to know he was—"

"Sick? Oh, believe me, I realized that right away." Londyn looked at her hand as it lay on the towel in his hand. "Can I ask you a professional question?"

Ice's head snapped up from his ministrations. "Depends."

Londyn looked toward the door and then whispered. "Why do you think he wanted me to submit to him?"

"He was in love with you, and I'm making an assumption, but I believe he wanted you to agree to make love with him so he could believe you loved him, too."

Londyn rolled her eyes. "Yeah, the beatings told me that."

"It's true. Come with me." Ice let her hand go. He walked to the door and turned back to look at her. Londyn turned off the oven, used a potholder to push the skillet away from the counter's edge, and followed him out the door.

As she walked behind him, she couldn't help but notice the breadth of his shoulders. He was a big man. Bigger than Bruce had been, yet she felt completely safe in his company. It was the same sensation as when she'd told Paris he'd protect them. The same concrete-firm acknowledgment that nothing could shake her belief that they were safe with him. It wasn't Stockholm syndrome. She wasn't lured into the belief. She didn't empathize with his cause. Heck, she didn't even know what his cause was. The connection she had with him was based on his actions, toward her and the things he'd done to protect them to that point. She wasn't a fool. She'd lived with a master manipulator for a year. Ice wasn't manipulating anything. He just ... was and that was what made him trustworthy.

Londyn turned to look at the open bathroom door. "Can we close this? I don't want Paris to see …"

"He's not in there anymore," Ice said, still walking.

"Where is he?"

"Gone."

"Just gone?"

Ice stopped and turned around. "Do you really want to know?"

Londyn stopped abruptly, so as not to run into him. She looked up and swallowed at the look in Ice's eyes. "Ah, no. Probably not. He's dead. That's all that matters." She rubbed her arms and winced when her hand reminded her she'd gotten too close to a hot pan moments ago.

Ice squared up on her. "You're safe. No one will hurt you. No one." He lifted a hand as if he were going to touch her cheek but dropped it.

She stared at him for a long moment. "I believe

you. I believe I'm safe when you're here, but what happens when you leave, or we all do? That terrifies me." Londyn blinked back at the mist forming in her eyes. "Damn tears. I'm sorry. I'm not a crier, or I wasn't."

"Remember those emotions I told you that you'd experience? The tears are a product of those." Ice's expression seemed to soften for a moment before he turned. "Come with me."

Ice walked into Bruce's office and then into the weird computer area that he'd had opened. He entered it, and Con, who was working in the first little domed area, turned. "Need something?" Con asked.

"Nope, showing Londyn the back room," Ice said and kept walking.

"You think that's a good idea?" Con spoke louder at Ice's retreating back. Londyn looked back at Con as she hustled after Ice. "I don't think it's a good idea, Iceman!" Con yelled.

Ice completely disregarded Con as Londyn scurried after his longer stride. He stopped at a closed door. "This isn't intended to scare you. But you need to see the extent of his psychosis. He was an aberration. One with the money and connections to get what he wanted." Ice opened the door, turned on the light, and then moved out of her way.

Londyn walked in. Her fingers flew up and covered her mouth as she stared at the thousands of pictures of herself. Monitors playing what she instantly recognized as her cooking and lifestyle channel were the only movement in the room. She turned, trying to take in what she saw. Shaking her head, she whispered to herself, "Why?"

"One could only surmise at this point." Ice was directly behind her, causing her to jump. She hadn't realized he'd moved into the room. "You were an obsession."

"I need to leave." She spun and moved as fast as her sore hip would allow. Londyn didn't think. She just moved. Con said something as she walked by, but she didn't hear what he said. The noise in her brain was too loud. She bolted through the living room and opened the sliding glass door walking out into the middle of the garden. Rain pelted her as she moved forward. She went straight for her tree and dropped at the base of the trunk.

Londyn dropped her head to her knees and concentrated on breathing. It was simply the only thing she could focus on at the moment. She sensed Ice as he sat down beside her. Still, she didn't look up. He waited in silence, and she appreciated the quiet. Finally, she lifted her head. "You don't have to stay out here in the rain." The dense canopy of the tree barely let any rain through to the ground, but she wanted to give him the opportunity to leave.

"I'm okay."

Londyn closed her eyes and dropped her head back until it rested on the tree trunk. "I'm not your problem, Ice. I'll be okay."

"I'm good."

She didn't really know what to do with the handsome man beside her. "I don't have the band-width to be polite company." She tried again to get him to leave.

"So, be rude. Be angry." He shrugged as if it didn't matter to him.

"Angry? I've been angry for the last year. I've lived on rage and hatred every day for the last year, Ice. I don't want to be angry anymore. I want peace. I want safety, and I want …" She lifted off the tree and leaned forward, picking at the grass.

"You want what?" Ice encouraged her.

"Nothing." Londyn shut him down. He knew enough about her.

"You want what? A family? A white picket fence? A husband who adores you, kids, and a cat?"

Londyn snorted and shook her head. "No. I'm not sure I ever want children. The world is so …"

"Fucked up?" Ice offered.

Londyn laughed. "After what I just saw, that description is exactly what I'd pull out of a hat."

Ice picked a long blade of grass and placed it between his thumbs. He blew through it, and the grass acted as a reed. A long, low, trilling whistle sounded.

"You agree with me, don't you? Sick people like Bruce … No one is safe. Especially children." She stared at him as he looked up at her.

"Once upon a time, I was as sick as Bruce." Ice stared at her as he spoke.

Londyn's heart skipped a beat as it jumped into her throat. She gasped, "What?"

"I had a brain tumor that pushed against my gray matter in a way it shouldn't have. I had delusions and saw and heard things that weren't there. The proper term is a psychotic break. I killed seven men. I thought they were after me, and I killed them with a gun I don't remember buying." Ice blew through his thumbs again. The whistle in the soft rain sounded melancholy and so damn alone.

Londyn turned toward him and watched for a moment, trying to digest what he was telling her. The fact that he killed someone didn't surprise her. She'd watched him kill Bruce and saw the bloody aftermath on his clothes when he'd killed the guards on the island. "Tell me what happened."

Ice stopped blowing and returned his stare to her. "Why? Interested in the morbidity of it all?"

"No. I want to understand what happened. I don't mean the killing. I mean the tumor."

"It was a slow-growing mass. The doctor who treated me in the emergency room ordered the tests that eventually found it. The surgery and the treatments afterward affected my personality. Or so people who used to know me told me." Ice turned back to his homemade whistle and made the sound again.

Londyn caught on the words *used to know me*. "Used to know you? Aren't they in your life any longer?"

Ice laughed and shook his head. "No, they're not."

"Why?"

Ice shrugged. "I didn't want them in my life. I'm

told I was a very kind man once. Caring, empathetic. You know, a typical shrink."

Londyn frowned. "You care."

Ice glanced over at her and then returned to looking at the blade of grass held between his thumbs. "Not as much as you think. It's almost impossible at times."

"You told me you cared." Londyn leaned forward and dipped down so she could see Ice's eyes. "Not in those words, but what you said meant you cared. You didn't lie to me." She was positive he didn't. It was a gut feeling, but it was strong.

Ice glanced at her and then busied himself with finding another blade of grass. "Something about this assignment is different. I can't explain that fact."

Londyn wouldn't let it go. She narrowed her eyes. "Why can't you explain the fact that you care about me? Am I that different?" Was she an aberration in his world? Something told her she'd like to be. To be included in the ones he cared for—the ones he protected.

Ice sat up and looked at her. He started to say something before he rolled his eyes. "No. I can't feel the way I'm feeling. The neurosurgeon took out that part of my brain. I'm done here. Can we eat that breakfast that smelled so damn good, or are you going to freak out more?"

Londyn blinked at him, shocked at the reminder of the room in such an abrupt fashion. She pointed in the direction of the computer area. "Don't you think I'm entitled to a minor freak out? Did you see what was in that room? He had pictures of me that weren't taken off the internet. He was following me. God only knows for how long."

"Okay, freak out it is. But remember, I'm hungry." Ice leaned back against the tree and put his hands behind his head. "I'd say he was following you for at least six months."

"Six months?"

Ice nodded and motioned to his head. "Your hair was longer in some of the ones by the door. The last ones of you before the photos turned to snapshots of you in this house."

Londyn's brow creased as she tried to remember seeing any of those pictures. Pictures of her in that house. "I didn't see those. The pictures of me, here."

Ice glanced over at her. "There were a lot of pictures."

"Yeah." She nodded and then lifted an eyebrow.

They sat quietly for a moment as Londyn bounced from thought to idea to supposition to anger to exhaustion. She landed on something she'd heard Ice say. "Do you think he had a tumor?"

Ice's eyes popped open. "What?"

Londyn cocked her head at him. "A tumor. Do you think what he did resulted from a tumor pressing against his brain?"

Ice stared at her long and hard. "I didn't tell you any of that so you could attempt to make fun of me."

Londyn frowned. "I'm not. Bruce was mental. Totally mental. A sick bastard. You said you were like him. I can't conceive a scenario where you were anything like him. You had a medical issue that caused you to act like you did. You can't put yourself in the same category as him or anyone like him."

Ice lifted his knees and dropped his arms over them, his back against the tree. "No. I don't believe Bruce's issues had anything to do with a tumor."

Londyn crawled closer to him. The damp grass stuck to her knees and hands, but it didn't matter. She sat down, her knees almost touching him as he sat at the trunk of the tree. "I'm scared, Ice. I'm afraid of what will happen when we get off this island. I want a life, one where I'm not afraid, where I can defend myself and pull the damn trigger if I need to do so. I want Paris to be able to live on her own and raise the baby she still wants. How do I even start?"

Ice leaned a bit closer. His intense stare should have been off-putting, but it seemed to reach into her soul and pull her closer to him. "I'll help."

Londyn lowered her eyes and almost whispered, "Won't you have to go back to work?"

He put his finger under her chin, and she lifted her gaze back to those mesmerizing eyes. "It's not like that. I only work when I'm required." His fingers caressed her cheek before he dropped his hand. "I'll make sure you're settled and secure before I leave you."

Londyn swallowed hard. "I don't want you to leave." He was her entire sense of security. Her peace was wrapped around and tangled up with the man's presence.

"You will." He cocked his head. "I'm still hungry."

Londyn barked out a very unladylike laugh. "Then let's go feed you." She stood up and extended a hand toward him. She watched as he leaned forward and, without the use of his hands, stood up. The sheer strength of that simple move reminded her of how lethal he was. A shiver drove up her spine, but it wasn't fear. No, it was the absolute knowledge that she was safe when Ice was with her. That sensation of peace was so foreign and yet something she'd been praying for. Now, the question was how long would it last.

CHAPTER 13

*I*ce stood by the beach and watched the waves roll toward the island. He felt her presence before he heard anything. "The island is secure, and you should be sleeping."

"I figured you'd do a deep dive today. I couldn't while it was dark. So, I'll join the rest of you on your schedule. I found an empty armory." Ronnie stood beside him. She wore her thigh holster, and he was strapped with enough sharp objects to slice his way out of hell.

"I moved everything."

"Con told me."

"I haven't taken the weapons out of the tree yet." Ice shrugged. "Best if they remain close."

"I agree." Ronnie sat down on a rocky outcropping. "Con said Guardian was going to get them help. The soonest they can pull a supercomputer away from what it's doing is next week."

"In the meantime?"

"In the meantime, we wait. I talked with the little sister before I came out to find you. The girl has had it rough."

"She has. Both of them have." Londyn wasn't pregnant, and she hadn't been violated sexually, but she'd been abused every damn day she was on the island, too. Ice pointed toward the water. "Shark."

Ronnie shielded her eyes and stared in the direction he pointed. "More than one," she noted as another fin appeared near the first. "Hopefully, all the evidence from this place is consumed."

"Do you care if it is or not?" Ice didn't, not even for a nanosecond.

Ronnie dropped both arms back to the rock behind her and leaned back, exposing her face to the sun. "Meh, it's easier on the organization when bodies don't wash up on shore. Sooner or later, they're identified, and then they show up here. Makes our life harder."

"There is that," Ice conceded.

"Londyn was looking out the front door. I

asked her if she wanted to come with me. Did you know she's never been out of that house, except for the massive garden in the middle?"

Ice glanced over at Ronnie. "I assumed. I didn't know for sure."

"Hmmm." Ronnie turned her face back toward the sun and closed her eyes. "They're coming to get me sooner rather than later. Archangel said he'd be delivering some help for you."

"Any indication as to why the women aren't going with you? And why are you talking to Archangel?"

"He's one of my points of contact when I'm on a mission like Fury or Anubis. Londyn and Paris will stay until you go off the island. Dr. Wheeler spoke with both women today while you were scouring this rock. Londyn was quite direct. She won't leave without you. Which is going to put you in a sticky situation."

Ice turned to look at Ronnie. "How so?"

"She's looking at you as her savior. You know, halo and all that shit."

"She knows what I am. She witnessed me taking out my target. I've told her about my … limitations." Ice turned again to watch the blue waves turn green as they rolled closer to the island, finally splashing on the rocky beach like a white foam.

"Really? You told her?" Ronnie sat up and turned toward him.

"So, you know?"

"Hell, yes. Tell me they don't brief you on limiting factors affecting the people you work with."

"Limiting factors." Ice chuckled even though it wasn't funny. "It hasn't stopped me from doing my job."

"I think it makes you better at the job." Ronnie stood up and brushed off her black cargo pants. "Why did you tell her?"

Ice shook his head. "I wish I knew." He felt a bond with the woman. Unlike any attachments he had with his friends. There was an attraction, too, sure. Londyn was pretty, and he'd watched helplessly for thirty days as that bastard got off by watching her on his damn tablet. But that sensation of … hell, it felt like ownership, and that was the completely wrong word. But still, in his mind, Londyn was his. He'd dissect that thought after Ronnie left and he was alone.

"Can I ask a question?"

If she ever decided to leave, that was. "Will it matter if I say yes or no?" Ice knew it wouldn't.

"No. How can you still laugh, joke, and have friends but not feel?" Ronnie picked up a rock and tossed it into the ocean.

"I have a sense of humor. That didn't go away. I know not to be inappropriate or overly rude. My mental functions haven't diminished. It's my *empathy* that has left the building."

"All right, Elvis." Ronnie snorted and chucked the rock into the waves. "So, how ... I mean, what is that like? How do you determine if there's a connection?"

"My friends are stand-up people. People that have proven I can trust them." Ice blinked. Well, hell, maybe he did use that term, as Jeremiah suggested.

"So, is there joy when you see them?" Ronnie asked as she picked up another rock.

"There's familiarity and a sense of belonging. Brooke, Flack's little girl, she's different. I miss her when I haven't seen her in a while. I'm lighter when I'm around her. That's surprising." He'd say he was more attached to Brooke than to anyone else in the world.

"Are you lonely?" Ronnie crouched down and grabbed another rock.

"Is this the South American version of an inquisition?" Ice reached down and grabbed a handful of rocks, too.

"No, this is me trying to figure you out. I'm interested in people in general." Ronnie tossed a rock, and Ice flicked a rock right after her. His went farther. Ronnie glanced at him and bent down to pick up another.

Ice snorted. "Is that so?"

"Yes." Ronnie flung the rock, beating the distance where his last rock had splashed down. "Don't you want to know anything about me?"

"I know what I need to know." Ice chucked another rock, and it splashed farther out in the waves.

Ronnie stepped to her right and flung the rock farther than he had. Ice ticked another box in his brain. "What do you know about me?"

"You work for Guardian as an assassin, but you've been separated from our class. That means you've got a background or perhaps a current issue that prevents you from being completely in the shadows. You're competitive." He lifted his eyebrows as he spoke.

"I am competitive," she said as she picked up another rock. Her lack of comment on the first part was more confirmation than denial in his book.

"You do this job, but it doesn't consume you because you're ... stable. You have a life outside this business. You'll kill to protect and to stop a monster, but you've never killed like the rest of us."

Ronnie dropped her arms to her sides and looked at him. "Why do you say that?"

"Manuel. You had a clear shot and didn't take it until I told you to do so. With the others, he would have been eliminated as soon as he grabbed the primary and the shot was clear." Ice whipped another rock into the ocean. "You're well educated, and I'd say well off."

"Defend that assumption," she demanded before kicking a mid-sized rock with the toe of her boot.

"Your language. Defend that assumption versus prove it." Ice chuckled when she rolled her eyes. "Your hair is professionally highlighted, and your clothes, while probably issued by Guardian, have been tailored. Your boots are handmade." She looked down at her boots and then back up at him. He'd surprised her with that one. He continued,

"The imprints you leave in the sandy areas." He pointed to the sand by the rock she'd been sitting on. "The sole is custom-made, I can't read the designer, but it's there."

Ronnie lifted her leg and looked back at the tread. Sure enough, the designer's name was present. "Guess I better change my boots. Not that the company has ever seen me, and I paid through a fake account …"

"Not absolutely necessary. Unless you're planning on visiting an island or leaving tracks." Ice shrugged.

"Never been to an island before, but I'll break in a new pair of boots that a million or so people wear."

"Always a good idea. Fade into the crowd." Ice pitched a rock.

"I'm going back to the compound to see if Con needs any help." Ronnie tossed her last rock and dusted off her hands. "Nice talking to you." She turned and headed back in the direction she'd come.

Ice snorted. "Nice being interrogated by you." He smiled as Ronnie's laughter carried back to him.

Ice took a seat on the rock that Ronnie vacated.

He stared at the waves and drew a deep breath. Londyn was his. He couldn't shake that feeling of possession or perhaps belonging. Rationally, he knew the last thing she needed was anyone claiming possession of her. Hell, she'd lived with that kind of crazy for over a year. Yet no matter how he examined his reactions because he knew it wasn't an emotional response, there was a distinct sensation of … ownership. Not like a car, more than that. The sensation weighed on him and was there whenever he thought about Londyn. Since his surgery, he hadn't encountered that type of event. It was disturbing and a bit unnerving. It had been a year since his last scan. Could the tumor be coming back? Was that what was causing the anomaly?

Ice swore bitterly. If it was, he wasn't sure what his course of action would be. Another surgery and perhaps another chunk of his sense of self gone. Hell, that was assuming the tumor was operable.

"Hi." Londyn's voice from behind him caught him unaware.

He looked over at her. "First time out of the house?"

"Yes. Well, except for the front porch this

morning. Ronnie told me to follow the path, and I'd find you."

Ice moved over, and Londyn sat down beside him. "I talked to Dr. Wheeler on Con's phone today."

"How did that go?"

She shrugged. "They wanted me to leave when Ronnie goes."

"And you said no."

"I said no." She pulled her feet onto the rock and looped her arms around her legs, resting her head on her knees. "I'm holding you to your promise."

"I made a promise?" Ice looked at her.

Londyn chuffed a small laugh. "You didn't make a pinkie promise, no, but what you said this morning, I know you meant it."

Ice nodded. "I did. Where will you want to go when you return to the States?"

"Anywhere but California and nowhere with cameras." She turned to look at him. "Any suggestions?"

Ice stared at the water. "I have several residences. You and Paris are welcome to any of them. You won't have to put utilities, rental agreements, or loans in your name. No one could find you unless you wanted to be found."

Londyn shook her head. "No, that would be a huge imposition."

"Not really." Ice pointed out just past the surf. "Shark."

Londyn straightened and shielded her eyes. "Wow. That's a big fin."

"I wouldn't go swimming in these waters," Ice agreed.

"I can't swim. I never learned," Londyn said as she watched the fin. When it went under the water again, she turned to him. "I don't have a way of paying you back. I mean, I can get a job. I was the executive sous chef at Le Petite Bistro."

"Do you want to work as a chef?" Ice asked.

"No. I … no." She placed her chin on her knees again. "I'll have to figure out something to do. A work-from-home job would be my preference right now. Will we have to testify about being here? About Bruce?"

Ice blinked at that question. "Not sure. I never see the other side of my assignments."

Londyn nodded. "I don't have any other options, do I?"

"About accepting my help? I'm assuming Guardian would put you up and get you back on your feet if you don't want to stay in one of my residences." He wouldn't push her to accept. The offer was there, and she had free choice. A heavy weight seemed to plant itself in his gut at the thought. He *wanted* her to say yes. He *wanted* her to come stay with him. He wanted to be the one to help restore her to the world. He *wanted* to be the one she turned to when she was confused or overwhelmed. And … that was worrisome. Those thoughts were as foreign to him as anything could be.

"No, not that. Testifying." Londyn pushed her hair that the wind had pulled from her ponytail behind her ear. "I don't want to be a burden to you, Ice."

"Burden?" He turned to her. "Explain that."

Londyn sighed. "I … I'm used to taking care of everything for Paris and myself. I have trouble accepting help. We'd be a burden on you. Financially."

Ice barked out a laugh. "No. You wouldn't be. I have enough money to support you and Paris for the rest of your lives. Money is not an issue." Guardian paid him well, and his parents had left him a sizable nest egg, which he'd invested back in his doctor days. He hadn't touched it, and the money had grown through all the market ups and downs.

"What about your wife? Girlfriend?" Londyn touched a small weed trying to grow through an almost invisible crack in the rock.

"I have neither. Nor do I have a husband or boyfriend."

Londyn glanced at him. "You're gay?"

"No." Ice shook his head. "Just no attachments."

Londyn smiled a bit before looking down and playing with the green sprout again. "Which of your houses would you suggest we stay at?"

"The one in Virginia," he said without hesitation. It was close to Flack's home, and Malice had an apartment about four miles away. He'd have people to watch over them if he were called to work.

"Then that's where we'll go." Londyn turned to look at him. "Thank you."

Ice shrugged. It was the rational thing to do based on the sensation that kept sweeping over him. He wanted to … protect … no, that was included, but damn it, he couldn't place a word on what his brain was trying to tell him. He'd get a scan as soon as he returned to the States. The ownership sensation scared the fuck out of him.

"Hey, Ice?"

He whipped his head around at Londyn's voice. "What?"

"I know you said you don't have empathy, but what you're doing for Paris and me is genuine and caring. Maybe you're not as disconnected as you think you are." She turned back to the surf. "This is really beautiful, overpowering. It makes you realize how small you are." She looked down at the green shoot, trying to survive in the inhospitable environment. Ice didn't know what Londyn's thoughts were, but to him, she seemed to be like that small seedling. Transplanted, she'd flourish. Left where she was, she'd wither and die.

"I'll take you away from here. You'll thrive." And when she was ready, he'd walk away.

CHAPTER 14

*L*ondyn stared at the little piece of life clinging to the crack in the rock. It reminded her of Ice. Solitary. She'd heard the hesitation in the doctor's voice when she'd said she wouldn't leave without Ice going with her.

"Why?" The doctor's question was abrupt.

"Because he'll keep me safe, and at this point, I don't believe anyone else can. I saw what he did here, and I've surmised the rest. He said he'd keep us safe even after we left the island. I'm not leaving without him."

"What about your sister?" the doctor asked.

"What about her?" Londyn was instantly defensive.

"She needs to be examined by an OB. She'll need

specialized treatment, as will you. The trauma you endured—"

"Dr. Wheeler, we've survived. We will continue to survive. We will leave when Ice does. Not one minute before." She put her foot down hard. It was their safety she was talking about. Survival. Instinctively, she knew Ice was that for them.

"You could be experiencing a type of transference where you think Ice is your knight in shining armor," the doctor objected.

"His armor isn't shining, Dr. Wheeler. Hell, I'm not sure he has any armor. I'm not in love with him, and I have no pie-in-the-sky thoughts of marrying him and walking down the aisle. But he is our safety, and right now, we need that more than anything else, including therapy. Believe me, we both worked with therapists after my father killed my mother and then himself. Safety is the basic necessity we need now. Maslow's Hierarchy of Need. Psychology 101."

A long pause settled between them. Finally, the doctor sighed. "I'll talk to management."

"You do that," Londyn agreed. "Did you want to talk to Paris?"

"I would. Yes," Dr. Wheeler confirmed.

"Hold on, I'll go get her."

"We should probably go in," Ice said from beside her, pulling her out of her memories.

"Do you think I'm wrong? For not leaving with Ronnie?" She usually trusted her instincts, but ...

"I'd prefer you stay." As Ice stood, he offered her a hand.

She took it, his warm hand wrapping around hers, and stood up. He stared down at her, still holding her hand.

"I'm attracted to you." He cocked his head. "I think you should know that."

She stared up at him. "I know you don't feel the things I do, but yes, there's an attraction on my side, too."

"I need you to be blunt with me. Are you attracted to me because of what I represent to you?"

Londyn stared into those laser-focused blue eyes. "Dr. Wheeler suggested my feelings toward you might be transference."

"He would." Ice shrugged.

"I think you're a very attractive man. I like you because you don't sugarcoat anything, and you don't treat me like a child. I trust you like I trust no one else, and I don't know why that is, but it's a belief I can't shake. Am I attracted to you physically? God help me, yes." She pushed her hair out of her face with her free hand. "And that sounds stupid after the year I've had." She looked up at him. She had to make him understand where she was, mentally. "He never raped me. He never touched me, other than the beatings. He was sick and manipulative, and I hated him. You took that away, and I'll be forever grateful, but I'm not attracted to you because you killed him. I'm attracted to the man you've let me see glimpses of. The man who told me his past when he didn't have to do so. The man who knew there was something off about Manuel and watched him like a hawk. The man, the one who is so intense he seems to suck the air out of my lungs, the man I like, and I want to know better."

Ice nodded once and turned to walk back up the path she'd followed down. Trailing after him, she hid a private smile at the fact that he was still holding her hand.

Paris was sitting on the porch when they walked up. Ice dropped her hand and allowed her to go first up the steps. "Are you okay?" Londyn asked her.

"Yes and no. The doctor asked a lot of questions." Paris looked between them. "Where were you?"

"Watching the surf. There are sharks out there. Big ones." Londyn sat down beside Paris. Ice didn't say a word as he walked inside the house.

"Talkative one, isn't he?" Paris nodded toward the door.

"No. I don't think anyone would call him that." Londyn took Paris's hand. "What do you think about living in Virginia?"

Paris glanced at her. "As long as it isn't California, I'm good."

"My thoughts exactly," Londyn agreed with her sister.

"The doctor said we'll be gone in a week or so. Long before the guards come back."

"I hadn't heard that. We'll leave with Ice."

"The doctor said I could leave with Ronnie tomorrow."

Londyn's head snapped toward her sister. "Are you?"

"No. I'm not leaving without you, and you aren't leaving without him." Paris bit her bottom lip. "I don't want you to get hurt. Don't let him hurt you, okay?"

"Oh, sweetie, I promise. I'm not in the same

situation you were. Those men and Manuel played you. They needed you to fall in love with Manuel so he could convince you to leave me."

Paris nodded and swiped at a tear. "He said you were safe. That you'd be okay, and I was the one in danger."

"We're both safe now." Londyn dropped her arm around her sister and took Paris's weight as the woman leaned against her. "That's all that matters."

They sat on the bench for a while before Paris said, "Virginia. It sounds like a nice place to start over."

"Not really a clean slate." Londyn chuckled sadly.

"No, but we'll get help, right?"

"We'll have help." Ice would be there. Paris's stomach rumbled, and Londyn chuckled. "Hungry?"

"Always," Paris said and sat up. "I'll be three hundred pounds by the time she arrives."

"Well, thank your lucky stars, you don't have morning sickness. Mom had it with you." Londyn stood up and extended her hand, which Paris took as she stood up.

"She said she had it worse with you."

"I don't recall that conversation." Londyn made a face like she was trying to remember.

"Right." Paris chuckled. "Come on. To the kitchen."

* * *

LONDYN SAT down under the tree in the garden. She leaned back against the trunk and looked up. The wind was moving the leaves, and now and then, she could see a star in the clear sky.

"Mind if I join you?" Ice said from her right.

She jumped and clutched her hand to her chest. "Dear God, you about gave me a heart attack."

"Sorry?" Ice said before sitting beside her.

"That wasn't too convincing." Londyn took a deep breath and let it out.

"Ronnie's transport will be here at six in the morning. Your last chance to leave."

Londyn turned and sat on her hip, leaning against the tree while looking at him. "Are we in danger if we stay?"

"Not that I'm aware of, no." Ice shrugged. "But that doesn't negate the fact that someone could fly onto the island unannounced."

"I'll stay. Paris had the opportunity to leave

with Ronnie, and she declined, but I'll ask her again." She wouldn't take Paris's choice from her.

Ice relaxed against the tree trunk with her.

"Tell me about Virginia."

He glanced at her. "I have an old ranch-style house there. It's been renovated and updated. Seven bedrooms, eight and a half baths. The designer called it a masculine-influenced country vision. I have no idea what that means."

Londyn chuckled. "I have no idea what it means either. Is it close to a town or a city?"

"It's located in the suburbs of DC, but far enough out you'd never know it. Close enough that you can get everything a big city has to offer."

"What does that mean to you?" Londyn asked.

"Ah, food," Ice said, and she laughed again.

"You have a food addiction."

"To good food, yes. It's one of the things that light up the pleasure center in my brain. I eat because that actually makes me feel good."

"What else makes you feel good?"

"Laughter," Ice said. "Laughter at Flack, particularly."

"Flack?"

"A friend."

"What else?" She let her shoulder touch his.

He glanced over at her. "Nothing else. Well, except for Brooke."

"Brooke?" A shot of something unexpected ripped through Londyn. It was akin to jealousy, but it couldn't have been.

"Flack's little girl. I feel good when I'm around her. She's almost three and has everyone wrapped around her finger."

"Including you."

"Especially me." Ice nodded.

"So, nothing else lights up your pleasure center?" Londyn stared at him.

Ice shook his head. "Not that I've found."

"Sex?" Londyn asked.

"I haven't had sex since the operation. Not even with my hand. Completely celibate."

Londyn sat up and turned toward him. "Is that due to the lack of desire?"

Ice took her hand in his and held it. Staring at her, he shrugged. "I'm not sure. I thought it better not to test the waters."

"Why?"

"Because I can't love anyone."

"You know what? I think that might be a load of pooey." Londyn swung around and laid her head on his thighs. "You love Brooke. You said it."

"I didn't say that." Ice's finger stroked the back of her hand that he still held.

"She has you wrapped around her finger, and you feel something. Although you wouldn't label it as an emotion, it's something you don't feel for anyone else. Maybe that's your version of love now." His thumb stopped for several long seconds before he started caressing it again.

"So, you're postulating that sensations I have that aren't assigned to anyone else would be my emotions coming into existence via an alternate route that my mind has devised."

"Um, I've never postulated before, but, sure, why not. I've always read that the brain can adapt and overcome obstacles. What did my therapist call it? Neoplastic something or another."

"Neuroplasticity," Ice supplied.

"Right. Maybe that's what's happening."

Ice made a noncommittal sound, but Londyn didn't care. She was finally happy under the tree that had listened to so many prayers and had been watered with her tears. She closed her eyes and drifted to sleep on the sensation of utter security.

CHAPTER 15

*I*ce knew the moment Londyn fell asleep. He stared at the woman as his mind recalled everything he knew about neuro-plasticity, which was next to nothing. Yes, he'd had a module or two in school, but as a cognitive behaviorist, he focused on transforming thoughts and perceptions to influence his patients' behavior. In the world of behavioral science, the field of neuroplasticity was relatively new. He could recall reading a couple of case studies about people who'd suffered the loss of limbs, experiencing sensations that affected the missing limb when they touched another part of their body. The one he could recall stipulated that one patient could scratch their face to relieve an itch on the missing limb.

Could his brain be rewiring itself? He thought of Brooke, of the lightness and energy he felt around her. He didn't feel that sensation around anyone else. Was it his brain's way of giving him the ability to recognize love? What about the possessiveness he felt for Londyn? Could that be a different type of love? A rewiring of his brain? And why would he sense it for Londyn? No, the idea held too many unknowns. He chuffed a breath out and shook his head. The more rational explanation would be that his tumor was growing back.

His phone vibrated in his pocket, and he sighed, moving to answer it. Londyn's eyes popped open, but when she saw him with the phone, she smiled, turned on her side to face him, and closed her eyes.

"Go," he said without looking at who was calling.

"What the fuck have you gotten yourself into now?" Malice's growl parted the connection.

"Screw you, asswipe. I'm on vacation on an island in the middle of nowhere." Londyn opened one eye and looked at him. He shrugged at her. She smiled and closed her eye again.

"That's what I mean. Dude, I was heading to the rally in Sturgis, and I got a call to hop on a plane. Guess who's coming to dinner?"

"Seriously?" He hadn't seen Mal in almost nine months. They'd been on opposite sides of the globe recently.

"As a fucking heart attack. I'll be there in the morning, your time. We're stopping to refuel now. Anything I need to be aware of?"

"No. Threats have been eliminated, and we're just waiting on the computer geeks to get things going."

"Yeah, I've got one of those with me. He's had his face buried in his computer the entire trip. He seems okay, though. At least he doesn't look like a strong wind would blow him away."

"Good to know. I look forward to seeing you, brother."

"And I you. Whatever it takes, my friend."

"For as long as it takes," Ice answered and disconnected the call.

"A friend?"

"Yes." Mal and he were tight. He trusted the man with his life, and that made him a stand-up guy. Ice rolled his eyes. Yeah, okay. He used that phrase too much.

"Why did you do that, with the eyes?"

"Dr. Wheeler may have made a valid point about something this morning. I tend not to like it when he does that."

"Why?" She moved and adjusted her head on his leg.

"I practiced for years in the same field as him. When I started working for Guardian and as I continue, I'm required to undergo evaluations. It's become a game. I think he enjoys it. Trying to trip me up … I make a point of not letting him."

A smile split her lips. "You're contrary, aren't you?"

"I've been told that before." He shrugged. "I'm not getting any emotional satisfaction from it, so it must be a personality trait."

When Londyn laughed, he glanced down at her. "What?"

"I can't imagine you any different from how you are now. I like this version of you."

He cocked his head and stared at her. "That's the first and only time anyone has said something like that to me." The heavy feeling in his chest grew. He stared at her and let a small hope that the feeling was an emotional reaction.

She put her hand on his thigh by her face. "I'm

sorry for that. I was thinking if I put myself in your shoes ..." She paused for a long moment. "But I feel like I've already walked a mile in them."

"What do you mean?" He was interested in the way her logic flowed. It was intriguing.

"Well, you know the person you used to be, but you're no longer that person. I know who I used to be before this happened, but I've changed. I've hardened and become determined never to be a victim again. And yet I'm more vulnerable and scared than I've ever been in my life. Do you feel vulnerable because of what has happened to you?"

Ice took her hand in his and rubbed the back of it with his thumb. The physical sensation was calming even though he couldn't feel any anxiety. A strange dichotomy. "Vulnerable. No. I don't have any vulnerabilities. I don't feel fear or anxiety. Frustration, well, that I sense very well," he admitted, trying to convey the complexities of what was and was not going on in his mind.

"That's a contrast in your emotional ... landscape, right? Strange how some emotions are still with you and some are gone. Humor and frustration still exist. And you trust your friends and your company," she mused. "There are remnants of emotions, and despite your surgery, you retain connections to certain feelings." She rolled onto her back, her head still on his leg and her hand still in his. "But it must be wonderful not to fear. To live free from the chains of what fear brings with it."

"It is difficult. Fear helps a person survive. To sense danger and be cautious," he said slowly, trying to allow her a glimpse into the challenges that came with his existence. He'd become an intimate observer of people, their movements, words, and actions. "I've learned to watch people carefully to examine their movements, words, and body language. I study my environment carefully. I tell people what I feel is gut instinct, but it's a learned skill." He wanted to give her an idea of his process of understanding the world.

Londyn turned back to him. "I never thought about it that way, but you have to, don't you?"

"If I want to survive, yes." He nodded, his gaze meeting hers with a quiet determination. He appreciated the depth of her understanding and the connection they were forming amid the nuances of his condition.

She stared up at him, and he held her gaze. That heavy feeling in his chest was a comfortable weight he was starting to welcome. "How dangerous is your job?"

He shook his head. "I can't tell you anything more about what I do." She knew. An idiot would know after what she'd witnessed and been told by her sister. However, he wasn't free to discuss anything else about what and how he did his job.

"Ah, secret agent stuff," she said with a small smile.

"Right. Let's go with that." Ice laughed with her. "Bond and all that shit."

"Is Ice your real name?" Londyn asked when they'd stopped chuckling.

"No." He hadn't even whispered his real name in over seven years.

"Can you tell me what it is? Just a first name."

"Zack, but that's not who I am anymore."

"Who are you now? Who do you see yourself as?"

Ice stared at their joined hands. "I'm not sure, but I hope to figure it out."

Londyn smiled at him. "You will. I have faith in you."

Ice relaxed against the tree and felt ... quietness. No frustration, no need to scan the horizon or be on guard. With Londyn in the garden, he let the stillness soak into his soul. He'd put his act back on when Malice showed up on the island. He was a different person with his team. They expected the wisecracking asshole who was a skirt chaser. If they only knew the truth. As much as he talked up the women when the other assassins were around, there was no interest on his part. Yet with Londyn … he felt things. His body stirred, and his thoughts turned sexual. He'd never hurt or push Londyn to do something she didn't want or couldn't do. He'd rather put a bullet through his brain than do that. She was special. She had somehow reached a part of him the doctors had told him was dead. At least he hoped that was what was going on.

CHAPTER 16

*I*ce stood by the helicopter pad and watched Ronnie duck under the rotors and run to the helicopter. Malice and a man were getting out as she jumped in. The men sprinted to where he was as the helicopter lifted off.

"Ice, this is Brando. He's here to help Con."

Ice shook the man's hand when it was offered. "Follow the wall, make a right, and enter the front door. Yell for him, and he'll find you."

"Got it. Thanks." Brando trotted off without another word.

"Good to see you, asshole." Malice pulled him in for a hug.

"Flack is the asshole." Ice pulled himself out of the clinch.

"No, Flack is the dick."

"Okay, then you're the asshole," Ice countered immediately.

"Probably," Malice conceded. "I got the initial brief. Sounds like the ladies have had a bad time. What's up with them not leaving without you?"

Ice crossed his arms and stared down at the toe of his boot for a moment. "About that. I have some information I need to give you. I'm not sure how you'll take it, but … I like Londyn. I told her I'd make sure she got settled and was safe. I've offered them my Virginia home."

Malice stared at him and narrowed his eyes. "I'm sorry, that isn't computing. What the hell do you mean you *like* Londyn?"

Just like his best friend to cut to the meat of the matter. The familiar feeling of frustration bubbled to the surface. How in the hell did he explain it when he didn't have a clue if it was real or a figment of his brain? "We have a … connection."

Malice rubbed his jaw with one hand, never severing their shared gaze. He opened his mouth to speak but stopped. Finally, he shook his head. "How?"

"Fuck if I know, but something's there. It isn't an emotion, but it's … there. That's all I got, man."

Ice shoved his hand through his hair. "I'm working on it."

"So, literally, you *feel* something for her? Like emotionally? I thought you couldn't. That's why you're a love-'em and leave-'em kind of guy."

Ice glanced back at the compound. "I'm going to tell you something else in the strictest of confidence. You have to swear on your life you won't tell a soul."

Malice's brow drew tight. "Man, you're my best friend. What in the hell? You know I won't say shit to anyone unless you start acting like a loon." An eyebrow lifted. "Like now."

"Ah, fuck you." Ice snorted. "Listen, all those times I talked up the women ... I never went home with them. I let you think what you wanted. I haven't been with anyone since my operation. I haven't had the desire to be with anyone." Ice stared at his friend, watching the disbelief, shock, and realization soak in.

"You didn't need to lie to me, man. I wouldn't have thought less of you." Malice put his hands on his hips.

"I didn't lie. All of you assumed. I never said I was with them, physically." Ice stared at his friend.

Malice frowned, and Ice could see him thinking

about the conversations. Malice's head snapped up. "Are you physically capable?"

"What? My dick is fine, thank you. Should I ask about yours?" Ice snorted as he gave his retort.

"No, I'd rather you didn't." Malice laughed and planted one of his meaty hands on Ice's shoulder. "Dude, have you told anyone upstream about the feelings?"

"Not yet. I will. I'm concerned what I'm feeling could be the tumor coming back."

Malice dropped his hand. "Any anxiety? Are you seeing people who aren't here? Feeling like someone is watching you?"

"No. None of that. It only happens around Londyn. I get this … sensation almost … that she's mine. It is a possessive urge … but that isn't it either. I don't understand it, and I'll talk to Jeremiah as soon as we ditch this rock. I promise."

Malice nodded. "I need you to be upfront with me, my man. If you feel weird in any other way, I have to report it. You know that."

"I know. That's why I told you about this."

"Damn straight. We don't want you to go all John Wick on us."

"I like those movies," Ice said. "Technically, that

guy's very proficient. Guardian should see if he wants to join up. I'd work with him."

They turned and walked toward the house. "True that. I dig the dog."

"Totally," Ice agreed. "Ever think of getting one?"

"A dog? Nah. I'm away too much. You?"

"Same. I was thinking of getting a Golden Retriever for Brooke," Ice said as they walked on.

"Oh, dude, I'll go in with you on that. Addy and Flack need to get her a pet. We'll just push the delivery date forward. Not like they wouldn't expect it from her favorite uncles."

"Addy and Flack can't refuse once we give it to her. We're golden," Ice punned, and they both laughed. Malice shoved his shoulder into Ice.

"That sensation you're talking about? Chase it, man. You deserve to be happy."

Ice wasn't sure that was true, but he planned on pursuing the chance after a brain scan.

They turned the corner, and Malice pulled up short. "Is that Londyn?" He nodded toward the beach.

"No, that's her sister Paris," Ice said and continued to walk. He looked back and stopped.

Malice was staring at the woman like he'd seen a ghost. "Dude, everything okay?"

Malice looked back at him. "Yeah, sorry, just lost in thought." They strode forward. "Let's go find the computer geeks, and then you can take me on a tour of your island." As he spoke, Londyn came up from behind where Malice stood.

"Not my island. Hers. Londyn, this is my friend, Malice. Mal, Londyn." Ice introduced the two.

"It's nice to meet you, Mal." She turned to Ice. "The new computer person is in with Con. I'm going to the beach with Paris."

"Stay out of the water," Ice reminded her.

"No worries about that." Londyn smiled at him and cast a quick smile at Malice before heading down the stairs.

"I can see why you're possessive. Nice lady," Mal said as he followed Ice into the house. "Damn, money put this together. Look at that. I saw it on the flight in. A fucking farm in the middle of the house."

"Technically, I think they call it a garden."

"Almost as big as Madison Square, if you get my drift," Mal chuffed.

"I do. I spent thirty days at the top of that tree on a platform."

Mal turned and made a face at him. "When did you learn patience?"

"I haven't. It was torture, especially because Londyn is a chef, and I could smell that food but couldn't eat it."

"Ah, damn, man. Is Guardian going to comp you for hazardous duty?" Mal elbowed him.

"They should," Ice grumped. "Here's the computer room." Ice nodded to the door.

"Fuck me," Mal said as he entered the massive chamber.

"No, thanks. I'll pass," Con said from the dome in front of them. "Thanks for bringing Brando. As soon as we get that supercomputer, we can process this shit and get out of here."

"Damn straight," Brando said from their right.

Ice nodded to Mal, and they walked to the back of the vast room. "The fucker that snagged Londyn was a sick mother." He opened the door and turned on the light. Mal looked in and did a double-take.

"She's lucky to be alive. Pervs like this usually kill their prey."

"I know. It gets worse. In the back is his spank bank." Ice turned off the light. "I let Londyn see this portion, not the back room."

"And the sister?"

"She was held in solitary for most of the year. The guards came up with an idea to kidnap her and get Londyn killed. They figured my target would pay for her to get her back. One of the fuckers gained her trust and knocked her up. She thought the guy loved her."

"Jesus." Malice sighed. "Sick fucks." He shook his head. "We normally don't see this side of the job. The after-effects, I mean."

"Right? I never want to do it again." They walked back toward the front of the house. "Get in, kill them, and get out."

"Preach it, brother," Mal agreed. "Show me around this rock."

"I thought you'd never ask." Ice extended his hand toward the door, and Malice walked out before him.

* * *

HOURS LATER, Ice and Malice had circled back to the beach in front of the house. The sun lowered in the east, and the reflection on the sea was vivid. "That's a fucking amazing view," Malice commented.

Ice glanced at the colors. "Bright," he agreed.

"Shit." Malice pulled out his phone and answered. "Go."

He listened intently. "Power. Hold on. I'm going to put you on speaker. Ice is with me, and we're alone."

After Malice put the phone on speaker, Fury spoke. "We've got a break in the case. The super-computer will be freed up the day after tomorrow. Con and Brando will work the systems until we have all the information our target has. Once that's done, your ride will come get you."

"Any activity from the security agency?" Ice asked.

"None. We have a man in country now. We'll know if anything happens. We've also been digging into the owner of the company. He's got dark roots and blood on his hands. Minor shit, comparatively speaking, but a douche, nonetheless. He's managed to avoid any prosecution. Prior militia and worked as a mercenary. The people he hires have criminal records, but according to our man on the ground, they're loyal. Money in this country goes a long way."

"They weren't too loyal." Ice put his hands on

KRIS MICHAELS

his hips and looked out at the water. They were going to sacrifice Londyn and kidnap Paris.

"Criminals, you can't trust them anymore." Mal chuckled.

Ice shook his head, and Fury added, "Where's the honor among thieves, right? We've got a net around you, digitally speaking, so you're not getting visitors without warning. Ice, I understand you have an obligation after this mission. You feel you owe these women something." Fury's question jolted him.

"I intend on fulfilling what I promised."

"That not asking permission credo again?"

"Probably," Ice admitted.

"You'll have plenty of downtime. This mission dragged on longer than any of us anticipated."

"Good. Also, you'll need to schedule me an appointment with Wheeler, and I need a scan."

"Symptoms?"

"No, nothing like that. I've briefed Mal, and he knows what to look for, but I'm good." Ice knew his responsibility to the organization. Now that the mission was close to wrapping up, he needed to get things rolling.

"Mal, take the phone off speaker." Fury's command brokered no objection. Mal picked up the phone, punched the button, and placed the device to his ear. Ice ignored the conversation and moved down the beach, so Mal could speak without him present.

He saw Mal turn toward him as he shoved the phone into his pocket. "Damn, son, warn a person next time. That was a grilling I didn't want or need."

"We'll be out of here in a few days. They need to know." Ice shrugged. He was used to his mental well-being being micro-managed. Some days, he managed to forget, but not often.

"Truth, but, man, couldn't you have told Anubis? That dude handles shit with less ..."

"Attitude?" Ice supplied.

"Rage?" Malice countered.

"Yeah, for an ancient one, he's still got the fire burning, doesn't he?"

"Truth." Malice nodded. "If we make it to that age, I plan on being mellow and retired."

"What are you going to do when you retire?"

"I'm going to buy a big ass cabin in the Black Hills and sit in front of the fire during the winter. I'll hunt, fish, and ride my Harley for the other four months of the year. Living life to the fullest."

Ice sniggered. "You need someone to snuggle up with by that fire, don't you?"

"Oh, yeah, man, too true." Malice nodded. "Somewhere out there, there's a hottie waiting for me."

"You'll find her."

Ice turned to see Paris coming down the path. She stopped a few feet away. "Londyn wanted me to tell you dinner will be done in about twenty minutes." She smiled shyly at Malice. "Hi, I'm Paris."

Mal stretched out his hand. "Mal. Nice to meet you."

Paris nodded and then pointed back at the house. "I'm heading back."

"That's one beautiful woman."

"Girl."

"What?" Malice's head whipped around.

"She's just turned twenty. Can't even buy a drink legally."

Malice growled under his breath. "Bastards."

"Yeah. Come on. I'll show you where you'll sleep."

"You know I don't sleep much," Mal griped.

"When you crash for your three-hour nightly

snore fest, you'll have a place," Ice said as they headed up the path Paris had just traversed.

"I don't snore."

"You snore like a freight train."

"No, that's Harbinger."

"Him, too. Where the hell is he?"

"Still bumming around Europe. He hasn't been back to the States in forever." Malice shrugged. "I figured I'd hop the pond and make sure the asshole hasn't gone stupid on us."

"Brass worried?"

"Not that anyone has said, but I am."

"Ah, yes. Momma Mal."

"Someone has to keep you fucking ducks in line."

"I thought that was Anubis's job," Ice quipped.

"Yeah, well, he doesn't know y'all like I do." Mal stopped at the steps. "I'm concerned but not worried. About you, and H. Fury knows that, too."

"I'm not asking you to tell me what you said to him."

"Good, because if you did, I'd probably have to report it. But since you didn't, I will tell you that I told him you were fine, and I've spent the entire day with you and not noticed anything different. Your worries about that pea you got rattling around in your skull aren't warranted, but I can understand why you want to get checked out." Mal turned suddenly. "God, what is that heavenly smell?"

Ice smiled. "That, my friend, is pure pleasure—Londyn's cooking. Let's get cleaned up. It's dinner time."

CHAPTER 17

*L*ondyn hadn't laughed that hard in such a long time. The banter between Mal and Ice was nonstop. Well, if they weren't eating, that was. She'd cooked more than she thought the six people on the island could eat, yet the men were scraping the platters as they helped themselves to thirds. Con and Brando had taken a plate to go, leaving just the four of them in the kitchen. Paris wiped at her eyes. She was laughing so hard.

Londyn glanced over at Ice, who was looking at her. She tipped her head toward Paris, who was talking with Mal, and mouthed the words, *thank you*. Ice shifted his gaze in her sister's direction before looking at his friend. He looked back at her and winked.

"I have dessert," Londyn said as she pushed away from the table.

"Paris, I'm going to marry your sister." Mal leaned back and rubbed his tight, flat belly.

"Over my dead body," Ice's reply whipped back at his friend.

"Man, I don't want to duel over cake."

"Cannoli," Londyn corrected.

"Okay, hold on, I need to find some white gloves to slap you with." Malice made a move to get up. Paris laughed and put her hand on Malice's arm.

"I don't think duels are necessary. We made enough for everyone."

Mal sighed dramatically and plopped his ass back down in the chair. "All right, but fair warning, I'll find those gloves. Can you cook like she can?" Malice pointed from Paris to Londyn.

"She's a fabulous cook. She made the lemon ricotta cream. It's delicious," Londyn said from the refrigerator, pulling out a tray of the pastries. The way Ice's eyes lit up and Mal leaned in, rubbing his hands together, was more than enough reward for the work she and Paris had put into the dessert.

"Half have shaved chocolate, and half are plain." Paris used the serving spoons and gave Mal and Ice one of each. "I'll take one of each to Con and Brando." Paris quickly loaded the plates and made her way to the computer room.

"You're a great cook," Mal said, his mouth half full. "So is she." He took another bite.

"Thank you." Londyn offered each of them coffee before pouring her own. "How long have you two known each other?"

"Too long," they both said at the same time.

Londyn laughed and shook her head, sipping her coffee before she tried again. "Okay, how long have you been friends?"

"Friends?" Mal looked up at her. "Damn it. When did that happen?" He looked at Ice.

"When I knocked you on your ass." Ice nodded his head. "Yep. Then." Ice nodded again.

Mal held up a finger. "Okay, well, first, that wasn't a fair fight."

Ice interrupted, "There's no such—"

"Thing as a fair fight, yeah, I know." Mal rolled his eyes. "Val kicked all our asses."

"Val?" Londyn keyed in on the name. "A woman?"

"No." Mal pouted. "She's more like an Amazonian warrior princess with ninja skills."

Ice nodded. "Truth." He took a bite of his cannoli and spoke around the confection, "She reminds me of you, or rather, you remind me of her. You're both strong." Ice tapped his head with his finger. "Smart and strong. You'll like her."

Mal's demeanor changed. "You think they'll meet?"

Ice shrugged. "If she stays at the Virginia house, they may."

"You gotta get clearance for that," Mal said, reaching for another cannoli.

"Do I look like someone who asks for permission?" Ice addressed Londyn instead of Mal.

She put down her coffee cup and leaned forward, studying him. A smile spread across her face. "No, you do not." The look they shared promised Londyn things. Things she desperately wanted. Things she'd thought she'd never have.

"And that is what gets him in trouble," Mal said before sipping his coffee. He rolled his eyes. "Even the coffee is fantastic."

Londyn took another sip before standing. "Time for me to tackle the dishes."

Paris walked in. "No, I can do them. You cooked all afternoon."

"Yep, I'll help Paris. Ice, take that woman for a walk or something. You need the exercise after all the calories you consumed." Mal stood and grabbed the platter with one remaining cannoli. "Oh, this is mine." Paris laughed and headed to the sink and the dishes Londyn hadn't finished before dinner.

Ice stood and extended his hand, which Londyn took without hesitation. "I've been told I'm fat. Would you care to join me for a stroll around the island?"

"You are *not* fat, but I'd enjoy a stroll." Londyn held his hand as they walked out the front of the compound. She'd never seen it at night. Small solar lights dotted the trail around the structure. As she stopped and looked back at the Spanish-styled building, a sense of loss settled around her. "This island could have been something special." She deflated. "But it will always be a prison."

As they started walking again, Ice commented, "I'll get into the safe tomorrow, and we'll find out what documents he's hiding. Anything legally indicating you as his wife will allow you to sell this place."

"Without his signature?" She glanced at Ice and stopped walking. "I mean, wouldn't I need a death certificate?"

Ice nodded. "You'll have everything you need. Guardian will ensure it."

"How can you be so sure?" She fell into step with him as he started down the path.

"I've worked for the company for years. Integrity is their hallmark. It isn't a word game with them. You became part of the family … ish when you signed that NDA."

"Ish?" Londyn chuckled. "That doesn't sound good."

"I promise it'll be fine. I know you don't have experience with Guardian, but they're a stand-up company." Ice made a sound in his throat. "God, I do say that, don't I?"

Londyn looked over at her escort. "Say what?"

"Nothing." He shook his head. "Let's go over there." He pointed to a faint trail. "There's a nice cove."

"Can you see?" Londyn tightened her hand in his.

He squeezed her hand. "Perfectly."

Londyn held his hand and carefully followed his lead. The shrubs opened up to a small inlet. Ice motioned toward a fallen tree, and they sat down. The waves were muted in the small space, and the gentle sound of them lapping at the sand was beautiful and relaxing.

"You're different when Mal is around." Londyn looked at the man holding her hand.

He shrugged. "I am who they expect me to be."

"Do you put on a front for me? Are you who you think I need you to be?"

"No." Ice glanced down at her. "You don't need any subterfuge in your life. You need truth and the ability to make decisions for yourself. The last year has stripped that from you."

Leaning on Ice, Londyn laid her head on his shoulder. "I enjoyed tonight. Your friendship with Mal is real and not superficial."

"Meaning what?" Ice asked.

"Meaning most of my friendships were superficial. People I used to know were fair-weather friends. The ones who wanted to be associated with me because of my success. And I know they wanted something from me," she groaned. "The women I was with the night I was abducted, I bet they didn't miss me for hours. They wanted access to the club I was invited to, so I asked them to come with me. Maybe I was trying to be something I wasn't. I don't know. But they scattered after the first drink. I was by myself at that table and had been for quite some time before someone sent over that drink. I took a sip. What a damn fool." Londyn had kicked herself every day for that stupid move.

Ice was quiet for a moment. "Slipping on my therapist's cap, I'd ask you why you thought that was foolish."

"Because I know better than accepting a drink from someone I don't know."

"You've never done that before?" Ice asked.

"Well, I have. Sure, but I shouldn't have that time." Londyn sighed. "Stupid."

"You know that now. That night did you know what was going to happen?"

"No." She lifted her head to look at him. "I wouldn't have taken a sip if I had. I would have run away. Or called the cops or something."

"So, you're basing your guilt and anger at yourself on hindsight. Would you do the same to Paris?"

Londyn frowned. "What do you mean?"

"If Paris unknowingly took a sip from a drugged drink, would you blame her?"

"No, of course not. She couldn't have known."

Londyn's brow furrowed. "But that's different."

"How?" Ice asked.

Londyn stared out at the water. "Because I'm supposed to know better."

"Ah. So, you're perfect."

"No, I just told you I wasn't." Londyn stood up and walked to the edge of the sand, where the water was spreading out in a light foam.

Ice came to stand beside her. "I think you should cut yourself a little slack. You were the victim as much as Paris."

"She was a victim because of me. You saw the room." Londyn sat down on the sand and took off her sandals. Stretching her toes to the water's edge, she let the waves lick at her feet.

"You were both victims. You did nothing wrong. Bruce did—simple fact. You can't take his guilt. It makes him less of a monster if you do."

Londyn looked over as he sat down with her. "How so?"

"Think about it. If you're taking the blame, how is he guilty? It was your fault. You did something wrong. Bruce didn't."

"Yes, he did. He orchestrated everything …" Londyn snapped her mouth shut. *Oh, damn.* As if a lightbulb clicked on in her head, she saw exactly what Ice was saying. She turned to him. He was closer than she thought, and she jumped at the unexpected proximity. His hands landed on her hips. He didn't hold her as much as steady her. "You're pretty good at this doctor thing. If the secret agent gig doesn't pan out for you, you might want to try it."

Ice looked down at her. His eyes moved from hers to her lips and then back again. "Do you want to kiss me?" she whispered, secretly hoping he did and praying at the same time he didn't. She wasn't ready for that. Was she?

"I don't know," he responded. "I haven't kissed a woman in years. I don't know if …"

"If you'll enjoy it?" She slid her hands up his arms, resting them on his shoulder. "We can test the waters. A small kiss. I'm not ready for more."

She toed up and waited. Ice stared at her for a long time before lowering his head, and then his lips brushed hers. A shudder of pure attraction looped down her spine and back up again. His kiss was light and chaste. He lifted his head and stared down at her.

Londyn whispered, "Did you like that?"

Ice narrowed his eyes and lowered again. That time, when his lips found hers, he licked hers, and she opened for him. God, he was so gentle and held her so tenderly as their tongues met and danced to a slow, sensuous tune only they could hear. Londyn followed his lead. When he lifted again, she leaned into his chest. With her eyes closed and her heart pounding, she absorbed the feeling of him and her body's reaction. She was equal parts terrified and ecstatic.

His hand moved up and down her back as he cradled her against him. She whispered her question again, "Did you enjoy that?"

Ice made a sound in his chest that vibrated under her ear and said, "Better than any food."

Londyn leaned back and looked up at him. Knowing he received pleasure from food, and it was his way of expressing his feelings, she smiled. "I'll take that as the ultimate compliment."

Ice smiled at her before dipping down and giving her another chaste kiss. "We should finish our walk."

"We should." Ice helped her put her sandals back on and took her hand. When they rejoined the primary path, he squeezed her hand. "Thank you."

"For what?"

"Understanding," Ice said as they walked down

the lightly lit path.

"I could say the same thing. I'm not ready for …" She sighed and looked up at him. "I don't know when I will be."

"And I don't know if I'll ever be." Ice stopped and looked at her. "I'm going to go to the hospital when we get back and make sure the tumor isn't coming back. The things … the sensations or whatever I'm experiencing could be my brain rewiring itself, but the more logical conclusion would be …"

"The tumor is back." Londyn put her hand on his chest. "I'll wait for you if you'll wait for me."

"I think that's an arrangement I can agree to." Ice dipped down for another one of those almost-there kisses. Londyn leaned into him, and he held her gently.

"You're an amazing man, Zack"

Ice chuffed out a laugh. "I had to think a minute. Maybe you shouldn't use that name. I don't think I'll answer to it."

"Ice it is, then. Either way, you've traveled a long road to get here, and so have I. Maybe together, we can find a way home."

His hand moved up and down her spine as he said, "I can think of nothing I'd like more."

CHAPTER 18

*I*ce watched Mal as the man made his third attempt to open the safe. "You aren't doing it right." He'd repeatedly tried to tell Mal that that model safe had a …

"Well, fuck it, then. Clyde, I'll be your Bonnie. Show me what I'm doing wrong." Mal moved out from in front of the safe and made a wide sweeping gesture toward what looked like an old-fashioned safe.

Ice lifted his eyebrows. All right, if he wanted to be a dick, so be it. He bent backward and yelled, "Con, did Brando bring what I asked for?"

Con appeared in the doorway moments later and tossed a black box toward Ice. "Here." The man left without another word.

Mal made a face. "They aren't very sociable, are they?"

"Meh, they're busy," Ice deadpanned. He pulled a super magnet out of the case and placed it where Guardian's message had instructed. The thing attached with a resounding thud. "Okay, come help me." Ice took two bars with handles attached to the loops on the top of the magnet.

"What are we doing?"

"Pulling. This way." Ice nodded toward the wall. Mal grabbed one handle, and he grabbed the other.

"Why?" Mal said as he braced his feet the way Ice had done.

"To move the bolt out of the solenoid. Ready?"

"Yeah, but why can't we use the tumbler?"

"Guardian's safe expert said this model has noise-deadening shrouds. You won't be able to hear the mechanism."

Mal dropped the handle. "You already knew that, and you let me try anyway?"

"I tried to tell you."

"Some friend you are," Mal muttered. He picked up the handle and braced himself. "On three."

"One, two, three," Ice groaned as he and Mal

leaned back and used all their strength to move the magnet from its position beside the tumbler.

"Motherfucker, we need a team of draft horses," Mal groaned.

The magnet moved a fraction of an inch. "That's it. Keep pulling." Ice strained with all his strength, as did Mal. The magnet slid and then popped off the safe. Ice and Mal fell on their asses on the floor.

"Well, fuck," Mal said, lying on his back and looking at the ceiling.

Londyn's call from the hall was loud and concerned. "Ice, Mal, are you okay?" Ice lifted his arm and gave her a thumbs up. He saw her face when she leaned over the desk. She blinked and then smiled. "So, what have you two been doing?"

"Opening the safe," Ice replied.

"More like killing ourselves," Mal countered. Ice sat up and looked at the door to the safe. It had swung open a couple of inches.

"It worked." Ice got up and extended a hand to Mal.

"No, man, you go ahead. I'm gonna take a rest right down here." Mal dropped his arm over his eyes.

Londyn peeked at the safe. "Can we look?"

"That's why we opened it." Ice swung the heavy as fuck door back and asked Londyn, "Clear a space on the desk for all of this, would you?"

He heard Londyn moving things as he reached in and grabbed the first stack of files. There was a box full of what looked like solid-state hard drives. "Mal, get these to Con and Brando."

"On it." The man was on his feet in a second flat. Two more stacks of folders and documents made it to the desk. "So, these are pretty." Londyn showed him a certificate.

Ice chuffed. "They should be. They're physical stock certificates." He took the certificate. "Issued from …" He drew his finger down the certificate and pointed at the company's name. It wasn't one he recognized. "They're new and registered, so they're probably valid, but most companies no longer issue physical stock certificates. Everything is digital."

"There's a lot of them here." Londyn fanned through a three-inch thick stack of certificates. At a hundred thousand dollars each, there was at *least* a couple million dollars worth of bonds. All registered to Bruce Jonas. So, that was his legal name or the name he bought the bonds under, at least.

Ice opened a red folder and stopped short.

"Here." He handed the wedding certificate to Londyn.

She dropped it like it burned her fingers. "I hate him. God help me. I hate him."

"When Guardian gets this, they can start finding and transferring all his assets to you." Ice shuffled through the other documents. Most were copies of transactions, banking, purchases of land, buildings, and vast company holdings. Jonas wasn't rich. He was filthy rich.

"Yo, Ice. Come in here a second!" Mal yelled from the computer room. Ice left Londyn to go through the rest of the documents and hustled into the computer room.

"You struck pay dirt." Mal pointed to the computer operators. Screens in two of the domes were active and scrolling like crazy. "One of those drives had the key they needed."

"Excellent. What can we do to help?" he asked Con, who was moving to the next dome.

"Stay out of our way, bring us food, and call Guardian to let them know we're in." The man sat down at the next terminal, plugged in the solid-state hard drive, and started typing.

"How long?"

"A day, maybe two," Brando said from a dome to Ice's right.

"Two. We aren't missing a damn thing on these machines. Everything is cloned and copied," Con snapped the words over his shoulder.

"Like I'd leave anything," Brando mumbled.

Mal chuckled. "Trouble in paradise?"

"Nope. Just a bossy older brother," Brando mumbled.

"Brothers," Ice mused. They had no physical similarities that would have led him to believe that.

"Did you find what you needed in the safe?"

Ice nodded. "Jonas was filthy rich. There's a wedding certificate, which means Londyn and Paris will have no worries for the rest of their lives."

"Good. They deserve a break. Speaking of which, is it lunchtime?" Mal rubbed his hands together.

"I thought I was the one who ate all the time." Ice followed him out.

"You do. Must be the fresh air here. Hey, Londyn, where's Paris?"

"She's taking a nap," Londyn said as she lifted papers and read. "I'll fix lunch in a minute."

"No, I can do that. You and Ice have stuff to do." Mal smiled widely.

Ice knew that smile. "Not again," Ice groaned.

"You got it, buddy. Grilled peanut butter and jelly sandwiches. The food of the gods." Mal slapped him on the back and headed to the kitchen.

Londyn looked up as Mal walked out. "He's joking, right?"

"Unfortunately, no. He doesn't cook anything except that and microwave meals." She grimaced and handed him a folder. "What is this?" Ice murmured as his eyes scanned the columns and columns of numbers. "Looks like coordinates." He took out his phone, pulled up Guardian's GPS, and entered one set. It took him to a small town in Iowa. He entered another set, and a small blip flashed halfway across the world in Singapore. "They'll go to Guardian along with all of this. Con and Brando are too busy to deal with anything else now."

"The rest of the paperwork is just like this. Titles and legal documents." Londyn closed the folder in front of her. "He was very wealthy."

"And now, you are." Ice started stacking the files.

Londyn leaned back against the wall behind the desk. "I don't want it. I want enough for Paris and me to live comfortably, maybe a college account for her baby. The rest … can Guardian use it?"

The dissociation of anything from the past year was expected, but in his opinion, not the smartest course of action. With time and perspective, perhaps Londyn would agree. She could do so much good with the money. Instead of speaking his mind, he took the paperwork from her and stepped closer to her. "We can talk about that later. You don't need to decide that now." Ice put his hands on her hips. "Don't let it stress you out. This is a marathon, not a sprint. We'll get through it one step at a time."

"I like that." Londyn closed the space between them and leaned against him. That warm heavy feeling in his chest burned a bit hotter. "I like that you said 'we'," she murmured.

Ice folded her into his arms. The sound of her voice and the memory of last night's kisses wound through him like the roots of an ancient tree, completely ensnaring him and taking all his resistance to an idea of a relationship far away. He sure as hell wanted more of everything with Londyn, but all of it, the thing between them, would come in Londyn's time. Not his.

"Are you ready to go back to the States?" Ice moved his hand lightly up and down her back.

She sighed and shook her head. "Not really. I … how do I go back?"

"Ah, that will be a process. People and events have moved on. You're still stuck on that night. It'll take time, but you'll eventually be comfortable in your own skin. I promise."

She leaned back and looked up at him. "I'm going to hold you to that."

"Please do. I'll do my best to make it happen."

Londyn toed up, and he dipped his head. He'd just touched his lips to hers when she pulled back suddenly. "Do you smell that?"

"What?" Ice was not even on the same planet at the moment. "Smell what …" The smell of something burning hit his nose. "Shit."

Londyn was out of his arms and jogging to the kitchen before he'd finished mentally cussing Mal out. He strode into the kitchen and batted at the smoke. Londyn was opening the sliding glass door with the smoking pan in her hand. She darted out of the kitchen and placed the pan on the grass about thirty feet from the house.

"Dude." Ice only needed to say the one word.

"I was trying to give you guys some space." Malice threw his hands up in the air. "Sue me. I've never used an induction cooktop before. That shit got too hot, too fast. It burned my sandwiches, and there's no more peanut butter."

Ice looked up at the ceiling. "Thank you, God."

Mal flipped him off.

Londyn returned to the kitchen and hit the switch to start the vents. "I think I'll take over in here." She shooed them out of the kitchen like they were wayward puppies. "Give me a half hour."

Ice pushed Mal out of the kitchen and looked back over his shoulder at Londyn. She smiled and winked at him. That warm feeling radiated through his body. He truly hoped his tumor wasn't coming back. He *finally* had something to live for.

CHAPTER 19

*L*ondyn stared at the small duffle sitting on her bed. She'd added a selection of necessities. Toothbrush, deodorant, hair ties, comb … She glanced at the closet filled with clothes she didn't buy and the dressers that teemed with expensive lingerie. She wanted none of it to come back with her. It was all tainted.

Paris walked in with her small duffle. "I'm ready." She sat down on the bed and looked at Londyn's bag. "What's taking so long?"

"I don't want to take any of it."

Paris dropped back onto the pillows and sighed. "I was the same. Mal said it wasn't the clothes' fault. It was Bruce's. Take two outfits to get back to the States. We can have a clothes-burning ceremony. Besides, Ice said he'd make sure we could get some new stuff."

"Ice and Mal were in your bedroom?"

Paris huffed. "No, they stood outside in the hall like there was a glass partition or something. They were working on the camera system."

A plume of anxiety pulsed through her. She glanced at one of the cameras, then the other. There were no lights on. She put her hand to her chest to keep her heart from jumping out and running away. "Working on it?"

"Yeah. Not in the house. They were making sure those were all off, except for the ones around the outside of the island. Con found the passwords and gave them to Ice."

"Oh." Londyn glanced at the cameras again. The utter violation of her privacy those cameras reminded her of was too recent to disregard. Her hand shook as she reached into the closet and grabbed two white blouses and two pair of jeans. She folded them and added clean undergarments before zipping up the bag.

"Mal said he lives close to Ice, and we'd see him around," Paris said when Londyn lay beside her.

"Mal says a lot." Londyn laughed. "Just never trust him around a frying pan."

"Oh my God, the house stunk, didn't it? That was the first time I ever threw up. Baby girl did not like that at all." Paris put her hand over her flat abdomen.

"You should think up a name. Baby girl is going to stick in our heads." Londyn lifted onto her elbow and looked at her sister. "Gretchen."

Paris shook her head. "Margaret Olivia."

"Momma's name." Londyn smiled sadly. "That's such a sweet thought."

"I'm determined to raise her the way you and Mom did me. I want to make you both proud." Paris smiled. "I'll figure it out."

"And you don't need to worry about a job. Bruce was very wealthy. We're set. You need to worry about staying healthy and delivering a beautiful baby girl." Londyn didn't want the money, but if it would alleviate Paris's worry, she'd use it.

"You're falling for Ice, aren't you?" Paris turned onto her side to look at Londyn.

Londyn stared at the wall behind Paris for a long time but finally nodded. "I am. He's different, real and basic, and so damn honest." Londyn sighed. "I'm done with people who only want to be around me for what I can do for them or who I can introduce them to. You know?"

"It was getting bad, wasn't it? So many fake people out there wanting their fifteen minutes of fame. Internet famous isn't all it is cracked up to be, that's for sure." Paris flopped back onto the pillows. "You can't trust anyone."

"You can trust Ice and Mal," Londyn replied without thinking twice.

"And Ronnie. Probably Con and Brando, too," Paris added. "They all work for Guardian."

"And we can never tell a soul about them or this place."

"Why in God's name would I want to tell anyone about what happened here?" Paris shuddered. "People are going to ask questions, however. Eventually."

"Ice told me if we were ever placed into that position where we were forced to say anything, to say we can't make any comments due to an ongoing investigation," Londyn repeated the words she'd memorized. "It scares me. Going back."

Paris's eyes slid to meet hers. "Why?"

"I … I'm not sure. Something to talk to the therapists about, no doubt."

Paris made a sound of agreement. "I'm scared, too. I'm trying not to think about being a single mom." She held up a finger when Londyn opened her mouth to talk. "I know you'll be there for us, but I also know I need to be an adult, her mom, and a woman of my own. I can't be the Paris they took, your little sister who let you do and take care of everything. I've changed too much."

"You have become more cantankerous," Londyn deadpanned.

Paris's laugh floated through the air, and it was the sweetest sound.

"Londyn! Paris!"

"In here." Londyn sat up on the bed. The alarm in Ice's voice chilled her to her core.

Ice sprinted into the room. "Come with me."

"Why? What's happening?" Londyn grabbed Paris's arm as they jolted off the bed on the side nearest the door.

"A helicopter is inbound. Not one of ours. Go to the computer room. We fixed the door. I'm locking you in there. Don't open that door until you hear Malice or me. We have to say the word *clear*. Got it? Do not open that door if you don't hear the word *clear*."

They all hustled down the wide hallway. "I understand. Everything is going to be all right, isn't it?" Londyn grabbed his arm and stopped him.

Ice glanced at Paris. "Go. Mal is waiting for you." Paris ran down the hall, and Ice turned back to her. "I don't know. I don't know who this is. We're damn good at what we do. I need to do my job now. Go to the computer room. Remember, do not open that door unless you hear the word clear."

"I understand." She toed up and kissed him hard. "Don't you dare leave me in that room."

"Not my plan," Ice said and spun her. "Run. Mal will get you set."

Londyn turned, and they jogged down the hall together. Ice left her at the living room, sprinting through the open doors toward the tree while she made her way to the computer room.

"Con and Brando are staying in here with you. They can't stop what they're doing. Find a corner and sit down. It won't take us long to deal with this," Mal said as he ushered her into the room. "Remember, do not open the door unless you hear the word—"

"Clear. I've got it." Londyn hurried into the room and spun to watch the door close behind her.

The clacking of Con and Brando pounding on their keyboards was the only sound in the room. Paris slid down the wall and sat on her butt. "Great. Now, I have to pee."

Londyn blinked at her sister, slid down the wall, and sat beside her. "It won't take long."

Paris nodded. "I've heard helicopters coming on days the guards didn't change. Three times. Who came?"

"I don't know. I was locked in my room. They didn't go into the garden, so I couldn't see them."

"So, now, we wait." Paris closed her eyes. "And think of dry topics. Not waterfalls or anything."

Londyn chuckled. Her sister, the snarky, loving person she used to know, chose a heck of a time to start to resurface. "Let me know if I need to start looking for a makeshift toilet for you."

"You're making fun of me, but you have no idea …" Paris rolled her eyes. "I can't wait to be off this island."

"You and me both," Londyn agreed. She drew a deep breath and prayed that whoever was on the helicopter wasn't dangerous.

CHAPTER 20

*I*ce put in his earpiece as Mal loaded two M4s that Ice had liberated from the armory the night he took out the guards. He handed Mal an earpiece exchanging it for a rifle. "Everyone up?"

Anubis's voice came through the earpiece loud and clear. Malice nodded at him as he worked to load magazines into pouches that would attach to their belts. "Roger. Arming at this time."

"You have eight minutes," Anubis said, and then the coms went silent.

Malice handed him his pouch, and Ice clipped it to his belt. He was more comfortable with his axe and blades, but all of them were expert marksmen. Their line of work required the best from each of them.

"Direction of travel?" Ice initiated the conversation once they were armed to the gills.

"Coming in from the mainland. Origin is unknown at this time," Anubis replied.

"You're sure they're heading here?" Malice asked.

Ice tapped him on the arm, and they headed out of the house and rounded the compound.

"The direction of travel puts them on a direct course to you. There are no other inhabited islands that we're aware of."

"Tourists?" Mal said hopefully as he broke away and jogged to the far side of the only cleared area on the island where a helicopter could land. Bruce had put the helipad too damn close to the compound. Ice veered to the left and pounded sand to the shrubs and cover that could camouflage him from sight.

"In your dreams." Fury's voice cracked across the connection.

"I've got better dreams than that," Mal quipped. "In position."

Ice moved a bit, gauging the route he believed

the helicopter would take. "In position. Take cover, Mal."

"I know what to do," Mal grumped.

"Then do it," Ice said and watched Mal disappear into the island's overgrown shrubbery.

"When you ladies get done fussing … Incoming in two minutes." Anubis didn't need to tell them. In the distance, Ice could hear the whomp-whomp of rotors as the aircraft made its way to the island.

Ice leaned around a tree and lifted his binoculars. "No registration numbers. Mal?"

"None on my side either. Blacked out. There's a gun mounted under the son of a bitch, though."

Ice diverted his field glasses and confirmed the weapon. "It's an M230 mounted under the nose. They're not here for a picnic."

"Standing by for Archangel's orders," Fury said.

The chopper circled the island and then moved to come in for a landing. "Guys, we're about to have visitors," Mal informed the people without a visual.

"Here's the orders. If they're armed, take them out. If you don't see weapons, hold to validate what's going on," Fury growled.

"Patience still isn't my strong suit," Ice grated out between clenched teeth. The black helicopter's windows were tinted so dark that Ice couldn't see into the bird. "See anything?"

"No," Mal whispered; although he didn't need to, the engine was still engaged, and nothing about the aircraft gave any indication that it was going to power down.

"Door is opening," Mal said, and Ice moved to the right so he had a visual on that side of the aircraft, too.

"What do you see?" Fury asked.

"Five targets, black camo uniforms, fucking body armor. Black helmets with full visors." Ice relayed the information as he zeroed in on the person closest to him. "All are armed. It took money to fund this."

"Hold," Mal said. "A woman. There's a woman on the aircraft. She's wearing a business suit. She's sliding across the seat."

Just as he said the last word, one of the men swung and looked in Mal's direction. The guard lifted his weapon. That was all it took for Ice to engage. He fired, intending to hit the man at the base of his neck. The armor the men were wearing would make hitting them in center mass worthless. It would bruise some ribs but not take the bastards out. Headshot if they had time. If they didn't, legs or arms to bring them down, and they'd finish up close and personal. His first shot missed, but his second shot fired a fraction of a second after the first hit his target. The muzzle flash from Mal's weapon registered as Ice pivoted and started shooting. Two more guards fell. Either his bullets or Mal's dropping them like flies. The helicopter started to lift, leaving the men on the ground. Ice popped several rounds into the front of the aircraft before he moved to the left and opened fire on the one remaining target.

The M230 engaged, and Ice dove to the ground and then scrambled to deeper foliage, not that the shrubs would stop a thirty-millimeter round from ripping his carcass to shreds. The firing was short-lived, and the helicopter veered up and away. Ice lifted his rifle and took another shot at the rear rotor. There was a faint trail of smoke as the bird zagged again and dipped out of sight. "Mal?" Ice spoke quickly.

"You don't have to yell, dude. I have my earpiece in."

Ice disregarded his petulant friend. "We have clean up."

"No, we don't. The gunner on the bird killed

them." Ice looked up. Mal was clearing the brush where he'd taken cover.

Ice stood and glanced around. There had been no hail of bullets. There was no damage to the foliage around him. Mal was right. The helicopter hadn't been shooting at them. They killed their own people.

"Sitrep," Fury demanded.

Ice did the brief. "Five down. We'll send prints and facial."

Mal bent down, grabbed a handful of black cloth, and rolled over one of the guards. "Not on this one." Mal moved to the next. "That gun doesn't leave much."

"Prints at a minimum."

"Weapons?" Anubis interjected.

"Russian made." Ice moved from body to body. "All Russian."

"The M230 wasn't," Mal said as he gathered fingerprints from the dead bodies. The app on their phone was a Guardian proprietary program. After each scan, Mal wiped the screen off with a special pad so the camera wouldn't transfer latent prints.

"Are you tracking the bird?" Ice asked as he helped Mal collect prints.

"Heading to the mainland. They've dipped below our ability to track them."

"Find out what airports will accommodate them in the general area."

"Already on it," a woman's voice responded. Ah, that was the one who hushed him the other day.

"Sending to Anubis. We're ready to receive the prints and any facial rec pictures."

"Standby. One more to process." Mal and he moved to the last body. As Mal processed the dead man, Ice went through his pockets. "No identification on anyone. No electronics."

"Check their ears," Fury said.

"Two don't have any left." Ice moved to the third. "Bingo." He pulled a large earpiece the size of an old hearing aid off the man's ear.

"Silent until you can get them secured," Fury bit out.

Mal rolled his eyes. Yeah, the ancient one treated them like they were two-year-olds.

They worked together to finish processing the bodies. Ice dragged the headless one to the beach and walked them out into the surf as he had with the others. If they washed up somewhere, the locals could deal with them. But with the sharks he'd seen in the area and the amount of damage to the bodies, they wouldn't make it far. Hell, the crabs would pick them clean.

It took a good hour to dispose of the bodies. Afterward, Ice took Mal to the armory, where they found an ammo can and deposited the earpieces into it before shutting it tight. "We're clear."

"We have local authorities on the lookout for the helicopter. Your extraction will arrive in three hours. Tell Con and Brando to hustle. They don't get any more time than that. We'll need you to destroy that computer room. Nothing can be reclaimed from the ashes."

Mal nodded at him, and he responded, "Roger that."

"Let's get to work." Mal headed back to the house. Ice followed. He needed to get the women off the island. The chopper that landed and the men that had deployed all signaled great wealth. Everything was top of the line. That helicopter wouldn't be the last visit. He glanced at the sky. It was time to get the hell out of Dodge.

CHAPTER 21

*I*ce double-checked the blasting cap. "You ready?" Mal called from the other side of the room.

"All set. Con, get your ass out of here."

"I need two minutes and ten seconds." The man stood beside the last computer; his laptop still attached to the machine. "One minute and fifty seconds." He looked over at Mal. "Brando's out?"

"At the helipad with the women." Mal nodded.

"One minute left. Give me this, guys, I've worked my ass off, and I'm not leaving without everything that bastard had."

Ice nodded at Mal when the man flashed him an irritated glance. "We can spare a minute."

Mal walked over to him and glanced at his

244

watch. "The documents from the safe are at the helipad?"

"Brando's got them," Ice confirmed.

"This has to work." Mal's eyes moved from explosive bundle to explosive bundle. "What was this guy storing up all this for anyway?"

"Probably this exact thing," Con said as he unplugged his laptop and shoved it into his satchel. "I'm out of here."

"Straight to the helipad," Ice called after him. They got no response.

"Ten minutes."

"I hope that bird is on time." Mal nodded and moved to the timer on his side of the room that connected four charges. Ice set the timer in the middle of the room and then the one on the far side. "Let's go."

They exited the room, and Ice reported in now that Anubis could hear them. "We're clear. Timer set for ten minutes."

"Chopper in seven," Anubis related.

"Fuck, that's going to be close."

"It won't take long to load us up and get the hell out," Ice said as they strode quickly out of the house.

"Did Con finish?" the woman asked.

"Yes."

"We're flying you into DC, and Con and Brando are taking a plane to my location. You'll have vehicles available for you. Do you need hotel rooms for the ladies?" she asked as they turned the corner of the complex and marched toward the rest of the people gathered at the edge.

"No. They have refuge," Ice said.

"Where?" Fury said.

"My Alexandria location," Ice responded.

"Copy," Fury batted back.

"Helicopter in five."

Ice and Mal stopped where everyone was gathered. "Five minutes." Ice looked at Con. He was the only other one who knew the computer room and half, if not all, of the compound would be destroyed.

Con nodded. "Brando, you got everything?"

"I do. This is our work, the hard drives they found in the safe, and everything we ghosted." Brando patted his bag. "The documents are there. We'll take them and deliver them to CCS." He nodded to the duffle bag that held them.

Malice grabbed the duffle, and Ice shouldered his backpack that he'd left in the tree and glanced at Londyn. "Ready?"

"I've never flown in a helicopter before."

"Actually, I think we have. We had to get here somehow," Paris quipped.

Londyn started to say something, but the sound of a helicopter approaching swung everyone's attention.

"We have a visual." Ice moved in front of the women and watched the chopper come in for a landing. The second it was on the ground, he took Londyn and Paris by the arm, and they ducked low under the expansive rotors while jogging toward the opening doors of the helicopter's passenger bay. Ice got them in and stood by the entrance to help the others. "Seat belts!" he yelled over the noise of the engine. He helped Brando in and then Con. Mal tossed the duffle in before jumping in. He reached back, grabbed Ice's forearm, and practically pulled him into the cabin. Mal shut the door and signaled the helicopter to take off.

The machine lifted as Ice took off his backpack and sat down. He'd just put on his harness when the first explosion rumbled under them. He glanced at his watch.

"What's happening?" He couldn't hear the words, but he thought that was what Londyn had yelled. Londyn leaned over Paris to look out the window. The second charge blew, and then the third.

Mal handed out headsets so they could talk to each other. He motioned for Paris and Londyn to put them on.

"Did you do that?" Londyn's voice over the coms didn't diminish the startled and perhaps frightened question.

"We did. We had orders to ensure nothing he had created down there could be used again."

"Good." Londyn nodded her head repeatedly. "That's good." She twisted in her seat to look back at the island. "I'm glad it's gone."

"Me, too," Paris said and closed her eyes. "I'm so glad."

Brando and Con opened their laptops and were furiously typing. Ice had no idea what they were doing, but the computer whizzes had earned his respect. Very little sleep and a hell of an effort. It would be a long time before all of the information, digital and hard copy, was processed. Or he assumed.

Brando turned the computer around and showed him the screen. It was a picture of the helicopter that landed. Ice leaned forward. There was a grainy shot of a woman with long brown or black hair that obscured her face. "We've got other pictures from the security system at the landing pad. I disabled it after this. Just in case."

Ice nodded. He had no idea who the woman was, but that wasn't his issue. Unless they sent him after her, which he wouldn't mind. Anyone associated with that island deserved whatever the Council sent their way.

They landed somewhere on the continent. Again, Ice didn't care where. He moved his charges to the waiting private aircraft. Mal made sure the documents were secured, and the pilots buttoned up the cabin.

"Galley is through there. We're fully stocked. Please stay buckled in until we level off and that light goes off. If you're sitting down, you're buckled up. Are we good?" The pilot lifted his thumb, and the ladies nodded.

"Good to go," Con and Brando said almost simultaneously, but they weren't looking at the pilot. They were already working on their laptops. Mal yawned and nodded. When the pilot looked at Ice, he dipped his head as well.

"We'll be in the air in less than five minutes. Buckle up."

Londyn's hand covered his. He flipped his hand

to hold hers. The warmth of her skin ignited that feeling in his chest again. "You're going home."

She looked over at Paris, who had her eyes shut with her head on Mal's shoulder. "No, *we're* going home." She looked back at him. "Thank you for giving us a home to go to."

Ice leaned over and kissed her, the warm heavy comfort of that feeling growing. Ice pulled away when the aircraft started to taxi.

"LADIES AND GENTLEMEN, we've been cleared to land in Virginia. Please make sure your seat belts are on. We'll be on the ground in less than five minutes."

Ice tightened his belt and watched Londyn do the same. Paris had used the bedroom to sleep most of the flight, and Londyn had slept against him—the feeling of her body against his sent that possessive sensation through the stratosphere.

The flight lasted eleven hours, and during that time, he'd drifted in and out, listening to Con and Brando exchange words now and then as the keyboards clattered. Mal stretched out on the couch and slept for five solid hours. That had to be some kind of record for the guy. He usually slept in snatches of a few hours at a time. He'd conditioned himself to do it when he was younger, and he either hadn't been inclined to change after Guardian had recruited him, or he couldn't.

The aircraft touched down and taxied directly into a hangar. One of the pilots exited the flight deck and opened the cabin door. Con and Brando were first out. Mal went next, carrying Paris's luggage, and helped Paris off the plane. Ice followed Paris while carrying his backpack and Londyn's small tote. He reached up and offered Londyn help down the steep steps of the jet. There were two blacked-out SUVs parked to the side. The other pilot crouched at the top of the steps. "Those are for the two of you. Keys are where they usually are. You've been instructed to check in once everyone is settled."

Ice saluted the guy and grabbed the document bag that had been retrieved from the underbelly of the aircraft. Mal headed toward one of the vehicles. "Paris, you can ride with me. Ice, I'm stopping for food. I'm sure no one wants to cook."

"Thanks." Londyn smiled tiredly.

"Come on, girl. What kind of food are you craving?"

"Fried chicken." Paris followed him. "And a milkshake. Oh, and I want a candy bar."

Mal turned around and walked backward, talking to Ice. "It could take a while."

"Take your time." Ice lifted a hand, and he and Londyn moved to the other vehicle.

"She'll be okay?" Londyn asked as Ice retrieved the keys from under the vehicle.

He scooted back out and sat up. "Yeah. Malice will keep her safe."

"I mean, what if someone recognizes her?" Londyn bit her bottom lip.

"The vehicles are blacked out. No one can see in. She's safe." He opened the passenger side door. She was silent on the ride to his house and only leaned forward as they turned down a long tree-lined avenue. Her gaze was on the imposing fences and massive gates that dotted the entries of the palatial entryways along the road.

She turned to him, wide-eyed. "You live around here?" she asked.

Ice nodded and pulled into a driveway about a minute later. He lowered the window and entered the fifteen-digit key to the security system. The massive wrought-iron gate rolled back, granting them access. It closed behind them with a resounding clank of metal against metal. "This is my Virginia home." Cresting the hill, Ice pulled down a long drive, and Londyn gasped. The expanse of the estate stretched out before them.

"It's bigger than the compound." Her voice was tinged with awe. She turned and looked at the vast lawn. "It's bigger than the island."

"Not quite." He bypassed the circular drive to the garage area located to the side of the main house. All the bays were full, so he parked the SUV under an overhang. There was room for Mal to park his vehicle there as well.

He gathered the bags and walked Londyn to the side entrance of the house. When he first looked at it, a sense of luxury seemed to be inherent to the property. He paid to have the lush gardens pampered and perfected. The air carried a scent of the roses that grew abundantly on the grounds. It was his mother's favorite flower, and he had many varieties planted. He opened the door and immediately keyed the code to deactivate his security system. "I thought I'd put Paris on that side of the house to give her privacy." Ice motioned to the house's east wing once they entered the main foyer. "My room is over here on the west wing. You can stay with Paris or closer to me." He wouldn't push the issue. Although he wanted her close, he'd accept her decision.

"Oh, wow." Londyn did a three-hundred-sixty-degree turn. "Travertine, marble inlaid stairs, wrought-iron banisters, and inlaid detail next to the crown molding. The slightly darker molding just pops." She turned again, slower this time. "You said you had a ranch. Ranches aren't two stories, are they?" Turning back to him, she seemed over-whelmed and twirled with her arms open, asking, "In what reality could this beautiful house be considered a ranch?"

Ice frowned. "That's what the real estate listing called it."

Londyn laughed and shook her head. "Beauti-ful. What did you say the designer called this style?"

Ice thought for a moment. "Ah … his mascu-line-influenced country vision."

"Yeah, boy, howdy, I can see that. This must have cost a fortune." She stopped and put her hand over her mouth. "Sorry, that was rude."

"How so? It wasn't cheap, but I like to be comfortable when I'm here." Ice had fancier places. His apartment in Paris cost three times the amount of this home.

"It's absolutely beautiful, Ice. Beyond anything I've seen before." She smiled at him. "Thank you for letting us stay with you."

Ice saw the chance to turn the conversation back to his question. "Speaking of which, east wing with Paris or west wing with me."

Londyn looked from left to right and put her hands on her hips with a sigh. "Paris wants her freedom. I should give it to her." She glanced over at him. "Don't you think?"

He put down the bags and stepped closer to her. "I think it's your decision." His hands landed on her hips, and her arms went around his neck.

"I've decided. We both need our space and privacy. I'll stay on your side of the house." She toed up. As he lowered, she drew back a bit. "But I'm still not sure when I'll be ready for more."

"I'm not rushing you. Everything we do is up to you." Ice dropped for a kiss, pulling her a bit closer after she swayed into him. The taste of her was addictive. The feel of her body against his was as perfect as anything he could imagine. She was built by the universe to be in his arms. He believed that with every fiber of his being. When she pulled away, he let her go after a few light kisses because his desire for her was manifesting in areas that had been dormant for a long time. He bent down, scooped up the luggage handles in one hand, and took her hand in the other. They walked down the hall, and Londyn stopped when he opened the room next to his. It was the champagne room—or that was what the designer called it. The duvet, curtains, rugs, and accents were champagne in color, but the floors, as was the furniture, were dark hardwoods.

"This isn't the master?" She stepped in and gawked at the fireplace in the corner with two champagne-colored wingback chairs and a dark coffee table.

"No, my room is next door." He put her small bag on her bed. "Through there is the bathroom. There should be towels and such in the cabinets."

"Oh, I'd love a shower." Londyn sighed. "But I don't want to put on his clothes."

"Then don't. Come with me." Ice walked out of the room and went into the bedroom across the hall. "Val left clothes here. You're about the same size."

"Val?" Londyn asked from behind him.

"She works with Mal and me. Her husband works in the area, and instead of rushing to buy a house, they stayed here and scoped out the region." Londyn nodded. "The Amazonian warrior."

"That's the one." Ice nodded.

"She won't mind me wearing her clothes?" Londyn asked.

"No. She isn't that kind of person. Besides she doesn't wear some clothes more than once. It's a personal quirk." He opened the closet and heard Londyn gasp. "Oh my God." Londyn scanned the full closet. "She just left this?"

"Yeah. I didn't care. No one was using the room." Ice leaned against the wall. "Pick something, and then you can shower. I'll do the same."

Londyn's eyes widened. "You're going to pick out some of her clothes?" Her laughter rang through the silent house.

Ice barked out a laugh. "Not in this lifetime. I meant I'd shower."

"I know." Londyn toed up and kissed him before turning back to the closet. "You're sure?"

"Positive." Val didn't care about material things. Sure, she wore expensive clothes, but the woman wasn't tied to possessions. Except for Smith, she owned that man body and soul. How Smith treated Val made Ice wish he could care that deeply— though it seemed like his wishes were granted. The warmth in his chest was an almost constant thing. At least when Londyn was near. He watched Londyn choose a pair of jeans and a simple top. She shut the closet doors.

"Thank you. I'll launder them and put them back."

"I'm telling you, she won't care." He tipped his head back toward her room. "We can shower before Mal and Paris get back."

"We?" Londyn asked breathlessly.

"Only if you're ready." Ice stared down at her.

"I…" She seemed at a loss for words.

"I know. Separate showers. Come on." Londyn followed him out of the room. He headed to his room.

"Ice?"

He stopped and turned back to her. "Yes?"

"I want to, you know. I want to be with you. It's just …"

Ice smiled at her. "I want to be with you, too, but there isn't a rush. I don't want anyone else, and I'm prepared to wait until my last breath if you need that long."

Londyn blinked rapidly. "Your truth. God, it slays me."

Ice didn't know what to say to that. "I don't know how to be any different."

She grasped the handle of her bedroom door. "I don't ever want you to change." She smiled and walked into the bedroom and shut the door.

Ice stared at the shut door for a moment. "I can't," he whispered and turned away. "I can't change."

CHAPTER 22

*L*ondyn slept all night and didn't wake up until ten the next morning. She stretched leisurely and made her way into the massive ensuite bathroom. After showering and donning the same clothes she'd borrowed last night, she made her way to the kitchen. The design and flow of the open-concept kitchen was beautiful. Dark cabinetry hid the refrigerator and accented the beautiful movement in the white granite counters and island. The four of them had sat around the island last night, utterly exhausted yet too tired to sleep—the hazards of flying through multiple time zones.

Paris was in the kitchen reading on a tablet. "Hey, I thought you'd never wake up."

"I don't think I've slept that long since I was fourteen." Londyn stretched, and her spine snapped and popped. "Oh, man. I'm getting old."

"Right. I'll get you a walker, Grandma."

"How come you're so chipper?" Londyn yawned. "Coffee." She scanned the counters. "There."

"I was lucky and scored the bed on the plane. I —I mean, *we* needed the sleep."

"You had a trump card. I would've wrestled you for it if it wasn't for my little niece." Londyn winked at her and moved over to the coffee station, where she chose a pod and a coffee cup from the glass-fronted cabinet. "Where's Ice? Mal?"

"Ice had a doctor's appointment. Mal went home last night after you turned in. He had to check in and see if his bosses needed him. He said he'd be back by today."

"Oh." Londyn frowned as she watched the coffee pour into her cup.

"Ice left a note for you. It's over there, by the microwave." Paris pointed across the room. "Man, who are these people, Londyn? I've never heard of some of these politicians." Paris swiped at the tablet. "I wanted to catch up on what we missed, but I'm not sure I do anymore."

"Yeah, it's probably better to catch up in small doses. Trying to review a whole year … I'm not sure I'm up to that." She sipped her coffee and walked across the kitchen to the envelope that Ice had left for her.

LONDYN,

I'll be back by four this afternoon. I didn't want to wake you. Guardian has scheduled appointments for you and Paris tomorrow. Paris, an OB appointment for the baby and therapy appointment for herself, and you for a physical to ensure you're healthy and then therapy. You can cancel the therapy sessions if you choose, but my past training tells me to ask both of you to keep them. What you went through needs to be dealt with.

As I wait, yours until my last breath,

I.

LONDYN CLOSED her eyes and held the note to her chest. The feelings she had for the man were so intense. So deep and strong that they scared her. How had he become so important so quickly?

"Are you okay?" Paris said from behind her.

Londyn jumped and twisted around. "I am. I just ..."

"You really like him." Paris smiled. "Believe me. I get it. Fortunately for you, Ice isn't using you." Paris moved over to the refrigerator and took out a bottle of water. "I'm so damn mad at Manuel, still." She looked up at the ceiling. "I loved him, Londyn. I really loved him. For me, it was real."

Londyn walked over and hugged her sister. "I know, sweetheart. I know. We've got appointments tomorrow. You for Maggie and then an initial therapy appointment. I have a physical and then my therapy appointment."

Paris hugged her back and spoke into her shoulder. "I need both. I'm worried about Maggie, and I hate hating him." She sniffed and then laughed. "I thought I was done with crying."

"I have a feeling we'll both shed a lot more tears before we're done."

"Great. Thanks for the happy vibes." Paris half laughed and half cried.

"Any time." Londyn held onto her sister.

"Ice, you deliciously stubborn brat, come hug me."

Paris pulled away from Londyn, and they both

turned to the entrance of the kitchen. "I bet you're in here. Always around food, aren't ... you?"

Londyn blinked at the strikingly beautiful snow-white-haired woman standing in the doorway. She wore Louboutin heels, blue jeans, and a silky white top. A long gold chain swayed from where it draped over her chest, and gold earrings glinted from her ears.

"Hi." She looked past them and then lifted the boxes in her hand. "I brought some pastries I made."

"He's at an appointment." Londyn stood in front of Paris protectively. "You have the code to the gate?"

"What? Oh, sure. I'm a friend of his. My name's Val." The woman walked, well, glided into the kitchen and set the bakery boxes on the counter.

"Val, as in the Amazonian warrior and the one who left ..." Londyn looked down at her clothes.

"Amazonian warrior? Is that what they called me? Brats. But yes, that would be me. My husband and I squatted here while we were looking for a place. We've moved in, but it's still a major construction zone. And you are?"

"My name is Londyn. This is my sister, Paris."

"Awesome names. Love that. How do you know, um …"

"Ice? Long story. He …"

"Oh!" The woman snapped her fingers. "You were part of his last mission. I need to start listening to Flack better. When he starts droning on, I tune out. Bad habit, but thankfully, it's just with Flack."

Londyn exhaled a breath she didn't know she'd been holding. "Yes." She nodded.

"Well, I need to hear everything." The woman put down her bag and moved over to the coffee maker. "We'll have coffee and eat the specialty pastries I made for Ice. The man loves to eat. You know that by now."

"I'm sorry, we can't say much about what happened." Londyn glanced at Paris. They had signed an NDA.

"What?" The woman glanced over her shoulder. "Oh, you probably signed an NDA, right? I'm excluded." She waved a hand with long, beautifully manicured nails in the air. "But, hold on."

Val went to her purse, pulled out her phone, and hit a number. She must have put the phone on speaker because Londyn could hear it ringing loud and clear.

"What? I'm busy." Ice's response was immediate.

"Screw you, sweetheart. I'm in your kitchen." Val walked over to the fridge and reached in, grabbing a container of coffee creamer. "Tell Londyn and Paris they can talk to me. I want to hear everything."

"You don't have a need to know." Ice almost sounded like he was laughing.

"Rubbish, I need to know, and if you don't let them tell me, I'll have Flack come over and do his lawyer thing on you." Val poured a dollop of creamer into her cup and put the container away. "Besides, I brought you pastries; if you're really nice, I'll save you one … or two."

Londyn glanced at the two boxes. There was no way the three of them could eat that many pastries.

"Londyn, you can talk freely to Val, but if she starts being a pain in the ass, tell her to go home. Is everything all right?"

"Everything's fine. We just weren't expecting a runway model to come through the door."

Val smiled. "Awww … You are so sweet. But seriously, I'm about sixty pounds too heavy to be a walking clothes hanger." She winked at Londyn and walked over to the cabinet to get plates.

Londyn glanced at Paris. "Six pounds, maybe," her sister whispered to her. Londyn agreed. The woman was stunning.

Ice sighed, "Don't let her bully you. She's a guest. You live there. Be nice, Val, or I'll change the access code."

The woman stopped what she was doing and looked at the phone. "Well, now, I'm insulted. I'm always nice."

"Shall we ask the team if that's a correct answer?"

Val tapped the counter with her long nails and made a face at the phone. "No, I'll take a pass. I'm hanging up now. I want a pastry and to get to know these ladies. I don't get much lady talk."

"Right, because you, Aspen, and Addy aren't joined at the hip when you're in the country," Ice countered.

Val snapped her fingers. "Oh, I should invite them over."

"No. Not today. Not this week, and maybe not this month. Some things need to happen before you descend on them. Give them time to decompress, Val, and I'm not joking about this." Londyn could hear the authority in Ice's voice.

"Okay ... Gotcha." Val grabbed the phone. "I'm

hanging up now. Ciao." She pushed the button and opened the top box. "Let's dig in. They are divine."

Paris moved over to the pastries, and Londyn retrieved her coffee before taking one of the flaky confections. "So," Val said as she sat down, "tell me everything."

"THAT LOOKS NICE ON YOU." Londyn turned at his voice. She, Paris, and Val were in the bedroom that Val and her husband had recently occupied. Ice stood in the doorway and cocked his head.

She walked over and spun in front of him. The knee-length dress floated around her legs. The material was divinely expensive and soft against her skin. Val told her that peaches and yellows were her color. Paris sat on the bed and played judge to her shopping through Val's closet. "Thank you." She toed up, and Ice kissed her. "Did everything go okay today?"

Ice nodded. "Why are you still here?" he asked Val.

"Oh, now, that's just rude. After we visited, these ladies told me they had no clothes, no makeup, nothing. I pulled in a few favors, and tomorrow morning at four—"

"Four?" Ice repeated.

"Yes, four. We don't want these ladies out in public. I'm sure Guardian will orchestrate a coming out event for them, but from what I've seen, the internet will blow up if they're sighted."

Londyn leaned into Ice. His hand landed on her hip.

"Anyway, we're meeting the district manager of a particularly large and established store with the best brands. The ladies will pick out a wardrobe, cosmetics, essentials, shoes, and purses—the basics. I'll meet you there. Bring your Suburban. You'll need it."

Val sat down beside Paris. "Then we need to get you set up with baby stuff."

Ice straightened behind her and shook his head. "Oh, no. I saw what you did to Flack."

"Poo, Addy will be in charge. She has baby sense. I have fashion sense. What time is it, anyway?" Val glanced at her Rolex. "Oh, dang, the afternoon has flown, hasn't it? Well, ladies, I've had a wonderful day, but I need to go pick up my husband from work." She stood up and strode over to where Ice stood. "I'm glad you made it back safely."

Ice nodded. "Thank you."

"I'll see you ladies tomorrow morning." Val waved her long-tipped fingers and glided out of the room.

"What did she do to Flack?" Paris asked.

Londyn turned in time to watch him roll his eyes. "That's a long story. How about we save it for dinner?"

"That works." Paris slid off the bed. "Is Mal here yet?"

Ice shook his head. "He'll be here shortly."

"Cool. I'm going to head to my room for a minute. I need to just chill for a bit. Val is intense." Paris left the same way Val had gone.

"That's an understatement," Ice drawled.

"She's a really nice person." Londyn felt compelled to defend her new friend.

Ice smiled down at her. "She's one of the few people I'd trust to be here with you. She's a stand-up person."

Londyn smiled, knowing that was a high compliment coming from Ice.

"What did the doctor say?" Londyn asked as Ice grabbed her hand, and they walked to his room.

He opened the door and guided them to a conversation area in front of a larger version of the fireplace in her room.

"The scan was the same as it has been," he said as he sat down.

"That's wonderful." Londyn sat down beside him.

"I talked to several doctors about the concept of neuroplasticity. It's conceivable that the brain can rewire itself. My knowledge of the field is almost a decade old, and while advancements have been made, any actionable information doesn't pertain to situations such as mine. The afternoon was spent pulling extrapolations and participating in a deep, scholarly discussion. The variables are too numerous to get into, but it was the consensus that my brain could be rewiring based on the sensations I'm experiencing."

"Emotions?"

Ice grimaced and shook his head. "No, not technically. Humor I still respond to. That seems to be the only real emotion I can, for lack of a specific word, ... feel. It isn't happiness, but the physical manifestation of humor and laughter *is* a pleasant experience. I feel it. It's hard to explain—the same with eating delicious food. I can sense the lightness. Frustration, I say I can feel, but as we discussed this afternoon, it's the condemnation I have with myself when I can't reach the emotion or reaction my brain expects. Not the emotion, but the result of my lack of ability." He sighed and shook his head. "I'm not explaining this well."

"No, I understand. When I would say a funny movie made me happy, you physically feel something, but mentally, that happiness isn't there. It's a lightness inside you, maybe?" She was trying desperately to understand the man who had come to mean so much to her.

"Right. I have a physical sensation, not an emotional response. When I'm with you, there is a sense of ownership." He tapped his head with his finger, and when he saw her eyes widen, he put his hand on hers. "It isn't the correct word to describe what I'm experiencing, but it's as close as I can get. When I'm with you, I feel a heavy yet comfortable weight in my chest, and physically, I respond to our closeness and intimacy. I haven't experienced any of those sensations before you."

Londyn stared at him for a moment and then smiled. "I understand." And she did. "I accept you for who you are, Ice. The emotions, they don't matter. That feeling in your chest? Maybe that's your heart telling you the same thing my heart is telling me."

He leaned forward and pulled her hand to his lips. Looking up at her as his lips left her skin, he whispered, "Until my last breath."

CHAPTER 23

*J*ce stood in the waiting room while Mal flipped through a magazine for the twentieth time. "Taking a long time," Mal said as he threw down the magazine and looked at the clock.

"They've been through a lot."

"Yeah, but they aren't going to solve all the issues today, are they?" Mal got up and stretched. The woman behind the window did a double-take and smiled shyly at him. Normally, Mal would have been at the window talking the woman up. Today, he just flashed a smile back and shoved his hands into the front pockets of his jeans. "Paris said the doctor said she was doing good. He gave her prenatal vitamins."

Ice nodded. "She's young and strong, physically and emotionally."

"Yeah, but damn, she's been through hell." Mal leaned against the wall a couple of feet from where Ice was holding up the sheetrock.

"They both have been," Ice agreed. A thought clicked into place, and he turned toward his friend. "Are you getting involved here, Mal?"

Mal glanced at him and then shrugged. "She doesn't need someone like me."

"Someone like you?" Ice cocked his head.

Mal threw a glance at the receptionist. Behind the glass, she couldn't hear what they were talking about, but Mal skirted the subject anyway. "In our profession."

Ice lifted an eyebrow but dropped the subject. He believed the profession wasn't as problematic as Mal's past. But his input wasn't asked for, so he kept it to himself.

The door opened, and Paris walked out. Mal was beside her in a second. "You've been crying." He put his arm around her, and she leaned into him.

"Therapy isn't for wimps." Paris pulled her new sunglasses out of her new purse and slid them on. "Better?"

"No, it would be better if he didn't make you cry." Mal nodded toward the door she'd just come out of.

"Londyn and I need a safe place to vent, right?"

"Yeah, sure, of course." Mal glanced over at him. "Where's Londyn?"

"She stayed back after our session together. Normally, it won't be this long, but we met with the doctor, and then she wanted to see us together. We can also do video calls if we can't make it in." Paris lifted a piece of paper from her purse. "I need to go to the pharmacy and fill this prescription." She glanced back at the door that hadn't opened. "Londyn shouldn't be long."

"I'll wait for her. Mal, when Paris is done at the pharmacy, you two can head back. When Londyn is done, we'll meet you there."

"That works for me. You okay with that, squirt?" Mal looked down at Paris.

"Yeah, but we need to stop for a milkshake. Chocolate." Paris smiled at him, still cloaked behind her sunglasses.

"Deal. You want me to bring you one?" he asked Ice.

"No. I'm good." Ice shook his head. He had another way to light up his world now. Food wasn't his only avenue to that sensation. He sat down and waited for Londyn. Fifteen minutes later, she walked out of the door, and Ice stood. "Are you okay?" She'd been crying, but not recently. The red and puffiness around her eyes had almost receded.

"I am." She paused before amending, "I'm going to be okay. Where's Paris?"

"Mal took her to the pharmacy to fill a prescription. They'll meet us at home." Ice opened the door, and they walked out of the office.

"Mal likes her, doesn't he?" Londyn slid her hand into his. Ice did a check, and yeah, that sensation was right where it should have been.

"Mal is a good man. He won't hurt her."

Londyn stopped and cocked her head at him. "That's not what I asked."

Ice winked at her and started walking. "I can't speak for Mal; I'm not him."

"And you're hedging." Londyn chuckled. "All right, I get it. I'll keep out of that relationship."

"Smart woman," Ice conceded.

"I am. And I'm a woman who needs to use the restroom." Ice ushered her into the elevator and hit the button to take them to the ground floor.

"There's one just before the exit," Ice said as the elevator started its downward rumble.

"How do you know that?" Londyn looked at him.

"I saw it when we walked in earlier." He saw everything. Every exit, every possible threat, every sideways look. Guardian was putting out a news brief that night that the ladies had been found and were back in the States. They would also put out a blanket denial of all interviews due to an ongoing investigation and ask for people to let them readjust after their ordeal. Ice had read the brief, and he'd made plans to stay at the Alexandria house with them for the next couple of months. Fury had granted that request immediately. Mal was still on call but, as of now, didn't have a mission. As far as he knew, Harbinger was the only one of them who was active. However, that could change with a phone call.

The elevator opened, and Ice guided them through the maze of hallways to the exit and finally toward the restrooms. "I'll wait."

Londyn rolled her eyes. "Go get the SUV. I can pee and walk out of the door by myself."

Ice shook his head. "No." He would wait right there.

Londyn turned to him and put her hand on his chest. "He's dead. He can't hurt me anymore. I have to start living again. I can't let fear stop me from doing that. Guardian is putting out the brief to all the news agencies. Go get the car, and I'll meet you at the curb." She turned and walked into the bathroom. He watched two other women follow her in and stared at the door. His gut told him to wait right where he was. The women who went into the bathroom were walking too fast. Ice moved closer to the door and found a position that wouldn't make him look like a creep staking out the women's room ... which was exactly what he was doing. He slipped into the darkness that lurked nearby in his mind. Everything ceased except for his concentration on that door.

LONDYN FLUSHED the toilet and adjusted her new jeans and shirt. The soft satin top was a light peach color, as was her handbag. She opened the door and walked into two women pointing their phones at her. "See, it *is* Londyn Chatsworth!" one of the women squealed.

Londyn tried to move past them, but they

blocked her way. "What happened? Why do the police still say you're missing?" The other one turned her phone and pushed it toward Londyn. Londyn could only see a picture of her and Paris that had been taken before they were kidnapped.

"I can't make any comments due to an ongoing investigation. Excuse me."

Londyn pushed past one, but the other blocked her way at the door. "No, this video is going to blow up. I'm going to have a million views."

"Two million," the other one said and flipped her phone, now filming Londyn, too.

"Let me out." Londyn raised her voice.

The door behind the woman blocking her way swung open, and she fell out of the bathroom, landing on her ass. Ice picked up her phone that skittered on the tile floor and stopped by his foot. He stepped over the woman on the floor and snatched the other woman's phone.

"Hey, you can't take that. That's theft." The one still standing tried to grab the phone back from Ice.

Ice grabbed the woman's hand, lowered his face to about three inches from hers, and stared at her. "Be glad you're still alive. Go away before you're not. Talk about her on social media, and I will find you. You do not want that. I have your phones."

The words were growled at a guttural level that terrified Londyn, and she *loved* the man in front of her.

He extended his hand toward Londyn, and she grabbed it. They hustled out the door. Ice's stride was so fast that Londyn had to run to keep up. He had her up and in his SUV and was pulling out of the parking lot as security came out of the hospital's door. The two women were with the man and appeared to be searching for Ice or Londyn.

Londyn's hands shook as she belted herself in. She ran the tape of what happened over in her mind. God, the way he'd growled at the woman. It was … Londyn blinked and then turned to stare at Ice. He glanced at her and then frowned. "What?"

"Nothing." She shook her head. But it *was* something. She loved him. God, she really did.

"Here, turn these off." He handed her two iPhones. She went through the process of shutting both off. Ice stopped at a traffic light and took the two phones from her. When traffic started, he tossed the phones into the oncoming traffic lane in front of a semi. Londyn turned to watch pieces and parts of the phones scatter across the three-lane road.

"Those were probably expensive."

"Serves them right."

"You waited for me." Londyn turned back to look at him. "Thank you."

"They followed you in too quickly. It wasn't right."

"I want nothing to do with the internet again." She pulled her fingers through her hair. "God, they were …"

"Wrong," Ice provided. "They were wrong."

"You probably made the blonde pee her pants." Londyn chuckled. "I would have lost it if I didn't know you."

"The act could not be tolerated." Ice shrugged.

"Were you mad?" Londyn asked.

"No, I don't get mad." Ice looked at her. "They put you in danger. My darkness responded."

"Is that what you call your anger response?" Londyn pulled her hair from behind her and tossed it over her shoulder.

"No. That's where I go when I work. The place where what I do doesn't matter."

Londyn turned so she could see him. "Like when you killed Bruce and the men on the island."

"Yes," he acknowledged.

"Do you ever go there when you're not working?"

Ice shrugged. "Occasionally, but only for a short time. During those moments, I remind myself I can return to that place."

"Have you been there when you were with me?"

"No." He shook his head. "It's a choice, a shift in my thought processes. If I ever go there without that shift, I need help." Ice looked at her. "Are you afraid of me?"

Londyn chuffed. "No. I think I'm in love with you."

Ice jerked the steering wheel when he snapped his head in her direction. He corrected their course immediately. "Say that again?"

Londyn drew a deep breath. "When you grabbed her arm and told her to go away, I thought I'd be terrified of you if I didn't love you." Londyn put her hand on his thigh. "I can't tell you when or how because it's too soon for me to feel this way, but I do. I love you."

Ice pulled over into the parking lot of a bank, slid into a parking slot, and stopped the vehicle. "I can't let you out of my life. What you give me … It's something I can't describe, but it's mine. I …" Ice seemed to search for words, and Londyn touched his cheek.

"You love me. The emotion isn't there, but the

sensation is. Your love, in whatever form it is, is enough for me, Ice. You are enough for me."

He pulled her to him, but she was strapped by the seat belt. Growling, he snapped the clip releasing the tether. She slid closer to him, and his arm around her back pulled her the rest of the way. The kiss was more intense than anything they'd shared to that point, but she didn't want him to stop. She didn't want him to be careful. She wanted to know how it felt to be loved by a man like him. The past be damned.

Ice broke off the kiss but held her close as they panted to regain their breath. "I talked to the therapist about us. About going further," she said, dropping her head to his shoulder.

"She told you no."

Londyn chuckled. "Stop being a shrink."

"Can't." He sighed.

"She told me that for my recovery, it would be better not to develop attachments to the man who rescued me. It might not last." She lifted her head. "But this, what I feel, will be in my heart until my last breath."

Ice lifted his hand and pushed a fall of her dark hair away from her face. "I can wait."

"I can't." Londyn swallowed hard. "I don't want

to. I want to feel you." She let her hand drop to his chest. "Tonight."

Ice stared at her with those intense blue eyes. "Tonight." He blinked and then looked at the parking lot. "And not here."

Londyn looked around. "Where are we?"

"At a bank," Ice said as he looked over his shoulder.

She didn't care. They could have been in the middle of the Sahara Desert for all she cared. The world had collapsed to just the two of them. "Then maybe we should go home."

"We should," Ice agreed and helped her get back to her seat. She put on her seat belt, and he backed out of the parking space. As he joined traffic again, he gripped her hand and lifted the back of it to his lips. "Until my last breath," he said, glancing at her.

Londyn held his hand all the way back to his home. That kiss on the back of her hand was his way of telling her he loved her, and she felt it through her very core.

CHAPTER 24

*I*ce had just parked his SUV when his phone rang. He pulled out the device and looked at the caller's identification.

He held up his hand for Londyn to wait as she exited the vehicle. She closed the door and looked at him.

"Go, I have Londyn with me."

"Affirmative, authenticate Snow."

"Frozen," Ice replied with his authentication code.

"Are you in a secure location?" Anubis's voice came over the connection.

"We're sitting in my SUV at my house. No one is around."

"Archangel, the connection is yours." Anubis turned the call over to the big man.

"Ice, we've been scouring the information we're getting off your target's computer systems. We've just scratched the surface, but we're concerned. His connections are beyond our understanding at this time. Most of the resources legally left to Londyn due to the marriage can be monitored and tracked. They could lead whomever he was working with to her. Guardian is prepared to fence the revenue and keep her safe. Several bank accounts can be liquidated and sent via shell corporations to her for her use, but it's one-twentieth of the revenue stream due to her."

"Sir, I don't want his money. I can get a job," Londyn said as she stared at Ice. He wouldn't let that happen. He had plenty of money. He could take care of her and Paris for as long as they needed him to do so.

"You won't have to do that." Archangel chuckled. "With the money we can safely get to you, you and your children's children will be set. But the rest ..." Archangel sighed. "I don't want to put you in danger. The criminal components of the entity Mr. Jonas was dealing with ..."

"Then do what you need to do with the rest of

the stuff. I don't care. I'm good as long as I can care for my sister and her baby."

"I'll have to send you documents to sign indicating you understand the totality of the revenue we will be fencing. When our investigation is over, and we've determined it is safe to distribute it to you, we will."

"Sir, it could be a trillion dollars. It wouldn't change my mind. I don't want it. Maybe Guardian can use it? You and Ice saved our lives. Use it to make monsters like Bruce pay for what they do to innocent people."

Archangel sighed. "I don't believe you understand the amount of money we're talking about."

Londyn bit her bottom lip. "Ice?" Her eyes lifted to his.

"Sir, send the documents, but I don't believe you will change her mind. If the transfer of funds has any risk, please don't. I have enough money to care for Londyn and her sister."

"The bank accounts we are focusing on transferring were under a pseudonym and highly protected. We think they were his emergency exit strategy. There is no risk." Archangel's words helped to still his racing thoughts.

"We'll send the documents but include a rider

that you may rescind your decision at any time once it is deemed safe to transfer the assets to you."

"That will be fine." Londyn smiled at him.

"I'll send you back to Anubis now. He has communication for you only, Ice."

Ice knew what that meant. "Affirmative, sir."

He took the phone off speaker and glanced at Londyn. "Could you wait for me by the door? I won't be long."

"Sure." Londyn opened the door to the SUV and walked to the house about a hundred feet from where he was parked.

"I'm secure and alone," Ice said.

"I apologize, Ice. I know Fury told you that you could stand down for a couple of months, but there's one that we've been put on standby for. It will be yours."

"Timeline?" Ice looked at Londyn, who was bending down to look at the roses on the bush beside the door.

"We've been given a thirty-day window."

"Climate?" Ice started down the mental checklist he used at the beginning of every mission.

"Ice and cold."

"Number?" How many was he supposed to take out?

"Unknown."

"Assistance?" *Please say none.*

"None."

"Just the way I like it. I'll be ready." Ice cleared the call and got out of the SUV, locking it with the fob as he crossed over to where Londyn was waiting.

"Work stuff?" she asked.

"I could be going away for a couple of weeks." He opened the door and punched the code into the alarm panel. "I'll give you and Paris the codes so you can come and go as you like."

"I don't think I'll be going anywhere after today," Londyn said as she walked toward the kitchen. "Will you be leaving soon?"

"Within the next thirty days or so. You don't need to be a prisoner here. That isn't what I want."

"Prisoner?" Londyn turned to him. "No, *this* is a refuge. I know that I can walk out that door at any minute. I know I can, but wanting to is another thing. After shopping this morning and the scene at the hospital, I'm about peopled out."

"You should have bought more," Ice said as he grabbed a bottle of water from the fridge and guided the discussion away from the women at the hospital.

"More?" Londyn laughed and moved up to him, putting her hands on his chest. "If I bought more, you'd have to build more closets in my room."

"Whatever it takes," Ice said as he lowered for a kiss.

"As long as it takes," Mal finished as he walked into the kitchen. Ice completely disregarded the man and took his time finishing the kiss.

"Awww ... isn't that the cutest thing you've ever seen?" Mal drawled when they separated.

"I think it's wonderful," Paris said.

Ice stared down at Londyn. Her cheeks were flushed, and her lips glossy as she smiled at him. It was a vision he'd lock into his brain. She gave him a reason to come back from the next mission.

"I'm going to make an early dinner. Shopping at four in the morning without anyone else in the store was fun, but I'm tired." Londyn headed to the fridge. "Paris, could you help?"

"Sure."

"You men find something to do, or I'll have you peeling potatoes." Londyn made a shooing motion with her hands.

Ice took the hint and left the room, bringing Mal with him. "Londyn was recognized today."

"No shit?" Malice dropped into a chair in Ice's

office. "Pour me some of that good bourbon, would you?"

Ice moved over to the bar and poured two glasses of amber liquid. "I'm on call," he added that tidbit, too.

"Shit, man. I'll take care of both of them while you're gone. I'll probably stay here if that's okay with you."

"Fine with me, but we can check with the ladies, too."

"Of course." Mal took a sip of the drink that Ice handed him. "Thirty-day window?"

"Yes." He nodded.

"Tell me something. The scan, it was okay?"

"Yes." Ice nodded. "I would have told you if it wasn't."

"I figured, but I wanted to ask. You and Londyn, that's going to be a thing, right?"

"Yes." Ice took a sip of the bourbon. He drank alcohol for the pairing taste with food or to be sociable. The effects didn't light up any pleasure zones in his mind, so he didn't seek it out like he did food.

"She understands about you? Everything?" Mal swirled the liquid in his glass.

Ice cocked his head and studied his friend. "I

don't understand the purpose of these questions. You know I've told her everything. What she doesn't know, she can't know."

Mal took a big sip of the bourbon. "Just conversation, my man. Val called me this morning. She and Smith are having a housewarming party in three weeks. She wanted me to ask you to bring Londyn and Paris. She's only inviting the team, so they'll be safe."

Right. Ice doubted that. Mal was working through something but obviously didn't want to share what that was. Something to do with Paris, no doubt. "I thought they were still in construction mode."

Mal snickered. "Smith put the contractor on notice last night. He'd had enough of the man ogling Val and not getting shit done. Val said it was a 'come to Jesus' moment for the guy. Things that couldn't be scheduled and finished have been miraculously scheduled."

"I would have paid to see that." Smith was a massive son of a bitch. The contractor probably shit his pants.

"Me, too." Mal chuckled. "Hitting the gym tomorrow?"

"Yes. I'll use the one in the basement and run in the neighborhood. I don't want to be too far away."

"I'll come over and spot you." Mal took another sip of his drink. "Climate?"

"Cold." Ice knew what Mal was talking about.

"Want me to pack your gear and bring it here? That way, you don't need to make a run into DC."

"I appreciate the offer, but I need to access other materials, too." His passports, money, and credit cards were all on the same floor of offices that he shared with Mal in downtown DC. The office building had the best security system in the city, and their floor was reinforced with a security system approved by Guardian. "I'll wait until I'm called, stop in for my gear, and then head to the airport."

Mal nodded. "They're probably sending you back to Russia. Lots of problems over there."

Ice took a sip. "I never speculate." He didn't care where he was sent or who he was told to take out. As long as Guardian was directing him, that concern didn't surface.

"It must be nice. I spin myself into the ground, twisting things around and wondering why, what if, how come." Mal finished his drink and got up, going over to the bar. "But then again, I always have."

"Momma Mal." Ice chuckled. His friend was always worried about something. Usually, it had nothing to do with Mal. He'd never let anyone know it, and looking at the man and his resting bitch face, no one would ever guess that under that *fuck you* expression was a guy who would do anything for his friends.

"You know it." The man poured another finger of bourbon into his glass. Mal didn't offer Ice a refill because Mal knew he'd refuse. They visited for about a half hour before Londyn called them to eat.

Ice could honestly say it was the first time since he woke up after the surgery that he didn't pay attention to the food on his plate. His mind was on Londyn and getting her alone.

WHEN MAL and Paris finally decided to watch a movie on her side of the house, Ice glanced at Londyn. She shot him a quick look and blushed.

"I'm going to bed early." Ice stood. He wasn't lying. He was going to bed early.

"I'll see you in the gym. What time?" Mal asked as he was leaving the room.

"Nine."

Mal stopped. "That's late, dude."

"You have somewhere to be tomorrow?" Ice deadpanned.

"No." Mal gave Ice a weird look before he stood up and followed Paris to the other side of the house.

Ice extended his hand to Londyn. She took it and stood up. He gazed down at her. "You don't have to do this if you aren't ready."

"I'm ready." She toed up, and he leaned down to kiss her, swinging her into his arms while their lips were connected. She broke the kiss with a squeal. "I'm too heavy!"

"No, you're not." Ice strode down the hallway and pushed open his bedroom door. He kicked the door shut and took her to the bed, laying her down on his comforter. She backed into the middle of the bed, and he followed her.

"You lead." He dropped by her side and rolled her on top of him. "You set the pace."

Londyn shook her head. "No. I want you to make love to me. I want to feel you, experience you. I'm not giving him the ability to take this away from us. Make love to me, Ice. Make me feel the way you feel." She put her hand on his chest. "In here."

Ice rolled again and lowered to kiss her. Her arms wrapped around his neck, and he let go of all the hesitation and doubt. Their kisses burned hot and wild as he discovered her body with his fingertips. Understanding every nuance of the beautiful woman would take years, but that night, he would try to memorize as much of her as his mind could absorb.

He trailed kisses along her neck and followed the path of her shirt buttons as he unfastened each of the small cloth-covered tabs. The ivory lace of her bra was rough against his tongue. He lifted the lace with his finger and licked inside the cup. Londyn's body arched, and her arms drew him closer. He finished unfastening the buttons while teasing her along the edge of her bra. Her hands found his hair, and she tugged him closer to her breast. He obliged by slipping his hand behind her back and unfastening the bra. Londyn sat up and threw off her top and the lace undergarment. She reached for his shirt and pushed it up. He lifted the button-down over his head and tossed it across the room. As her hands found his belt buckle and unfastened it, he moved down and kissed her, dropping her onto the bed again. Her hands explored his chest as he kissed her. Their tongues tangled in a dance neither knew, and both were able to perform flawlessly. He broke away and lowered to her breasts. The gasping sounds she made fueled the heat in his chest. His mind was alive with brilliant and undeniable flashes of pleasure.

He kissed his way down to her jeans and unfastened the button. Grabbing the zipper tab with his teeth, he pulled it down. Londyn propped up on her elbows to watch. The rose-colored tips of her breasts were taut with excitement. Her hair sprayed across her shoulders, and her lips were swollen. She was extraordinarily beautiful.

He lifted and moved to the end of the bed, where he took off her shoes and grabbed the bottom of her jeans. With a slow tug, he inched her jeans off. The small strip of lace that covered her sex was like a red flag to a raging bull. He ran his hands up her legs and grabbed the lace, sliding it down her legs. God, she was magnificent.

"Your turn." Londyn's hoarse voice jolted him from his admiration. He toed off his boots and stripped out of his clothes. His cock was heavy with need and stood out proudly in front of him. He picked up his jeans, grabbed his wallet, and took out a condom. Ice quickly rolled the thing on before he moved over her again. She reached for his shaft, but he stopped her.

"It's been too long. I won't last." He bent down and kissed her. "Let me take care of you first."

Sex was truly a physical act. Scientifically, he knew it, but what they were doing was transcending that for him. He understood the chemistry but couldn't fathom the intensity of the sensations traveling at warp speed through his body. He was shaking, and his heart was pounding out of his chest as he discovered her body. The swell of her breasts, the curve of her hips, and the lush heat of her sex clouded any thoughts out of his mind. He became the experience. He became the rush of blood under his skin and the heat of his desire.

"Please, now. I need you in me now," Londyn begged.

Ice moved forward and centered himself. Londyn was hot and ready for him. As he slid inside her body, his eyes rolled back in his head. Explosions of sensation completely voided any cognitive thought. Her arms pulled him back down, and he adjusted to move inside her. Ice found her shoulder and buried his brow against her neck. Her legs wrapped around his waist, and she arched and tightened around him. A torrent of feeling sucked him over the edge less than a minute after he'd entered her.

He trembled as he held himself off her and sucked in air. He felt her push his sweaty hair back from his brow and opened his eyes to stare at her. "You're amazing." Her arm flopped out to the side. He dropped onto his shoulder in the other direction, taking care of the condom and tossing it in the trash beside the bed before pulling her into his arms. "I'm sorry."

She stiffened. "For what?"

"Not lasting longer."

Londyn laughed and lifted her head to look at the bedside table. "You teased and tempted me for almost an hour. I was ready. I'm not complaining."

Ice glanced at the clock. He had no idea that much time had passed. Londyn sighed and moved closer to him. "Was it good for you?"

Ice gathered her into his arms. "I'm trying to find the words. I ... found me for a short time. I can't say I felt euphoria, but the manifestation was as close to that as I think I can get."

Londyn arched back, and he looked down at her to see her smiling. "So, sex was good for you?"

Ice rolled his eyes. "It was better than good. That's what I'm trying to tell you."

She laughed and tucked her head under his chin. "I think we're good together."

Ice stroked her back with his fingers. "I think we belong together."

She nodded and yawned. "Until our last breath."

CHAPTER 25

 *ive months later:*

HARBINGER WHISTLED when Ice pulled up to his Virginia home. Londyn and Paris had decorated the tree they could see in the living room window with Christmas lights. It was an impressive display. Of course, Ice had spent most of the weekend before he went to the Rose hanging upside-down from the roof with a staple gun hanging outdoor lights. Thank God he was flexible and strong. A couple of times, he thought he would end up in the rose bushes that circled the house. "Nice place, man."

"Well, if you were ever in the States, you'd have

been here before." Ice put the SUV into Park, and they grabbed their bags. They'd spent the last two weeks at the Rose going through training and meeting the new class. Eight of the most ragtag crew he'd ever seen. Still, he remembered when he and the others had started training. There was a hell of a lot of personalities involved. That old saying you don't spell team with an I? Well, when they started, their team had seven of those suckers. The training had morphed them into a team, and he was damn glad it had. His team was his family.

"What's with all the cars?"

Ice had clocked them as they drove in. He pointed to each one. "That's Flack's Cadillac." The one he'd bought for the guy when Brooke had come to live with him. "Val and Smith's Bentley, Phoenix and Aspen's Lincoln, that's Smoke and Charley's Guardian vehicle, and the rental is probably Reaper and Harmony's. The car seat is a dead giveaway. Mal's car is probably in the garage." He noticed his old work truck was parked outside.

Harbinger stopped. "The whole team is here? What's the reason?"

Ice turned to look at him. "I'd say it is because of you."

Harbinger shook his head. "Stay away a couple of years, and people get sappy."

"I don't get sappy," Ice corrected him.

"Well, that's true." Harbinger chuckled.

Ice opened the side door, and they dropped their bags in the hall. He shut the door and heard a bout of laughter. "They're probably in the kitchen."

"God, if that amazing smell is coming from the kitchen, that's where I'm heading, too." Harbinger rubbed his hands together and headed into the house. Ice grabbed his shoulder and turned him in the right direction at the foyer.

"Well, look who finally came back into the fold." Smoke walked up to Harbinger and grabbed him in a massive hug. He grabbed Harbinger's shoulders and shoved him out to look at him. "We're making a policy change that all team members need to be back stateside at least two months out of the year."

Harbinger's face was priceless. His eyes widened, and he looked toward Ice for confirmation since Ice didn't lie. Ice rolled his eyes, and Smoke burst into laughter.

Londyn slid through the crowd and jogged over to him. Ice caught her and bent down to kiss her. The crowd hooted and hollered, giving a couple of whistles. Londyn was laughing when he backed away. "I missed you."

"I missed you more." Londyn had become the center of his universe and grounded him in a way nothing or no one could after the surgery.

"Wait a minute. Wait a wet-dog stinking minute. When did this happen?" Harbinger pointed to Londyn and him.

"Where the hel … heck have you been?" Phoenix asked and mouthed sorry to Reaper because his kid was there too.

Reaper winked at him. Flack picked up Brooke and bounced her.

Brooke twisted and squealed, "Uncle Ith!"

Ice grabbed the child and tossed her into the air. The little girl giggled and wrapped her arms around Ice's neck as Ice patted her back.

"She's heard worse, but we appreciate the self-edit." Flack clasped Phoenix on the shoulder.

"H. has been in Europe. We all know this." Val shrugged. "But if you can't be bothered to come home, you can't have the gossip."

"That's the truth." Reaper held his daughter Iris and put his arm around Harmony, who was pregnant with their second child.

"Wow, congratulations, you two." Harbinger

walked over and shook Reaper's hand, then hugged Harmony. "Seriously, though." He turned and pointed at Londyn and Ice. "Someone had better start explaining. I didn't think this was possible?"

Charley grabbed her wine and took Harbinger by the arm. "Let's get you a drink, and I'll catch you up."

Harbinger smiled down at Charley. "You're Smoke's wife, right?"

"Correct, and they said you weren't the sharpest tack in the box." Laughter erupted, and the crowd filed out after Charley and Harbinger. Flack clapped his hands and spread them out, and Brooke dove to her father. Ice put his arm around Londyn when Brooke was secure in Flack's arms. They met up with Addy in the hall and headed toward the living room.

Val and Smith stayed behind. "Can we do anything to help, Londyn?"

"No, thank you so … Oh, wait." She skittered over to the refrigerator. "Can you take these out to them? Dinner is still another forty-five minutes." Londyn pulled out a tray of hors d'oeuvres. Smith took the platter, and Val grabbed plates and napkins.

"On it," Val said as she followed Smith to the living room.

Londyn shut the refrigerator door. "Paris and Mal will be right back with the heavy cream I need for the potatoes."

Ice made his way over to Londyn. "I thought the party was tomorrow night." He wrapped her in his arms.

"Phoenix has business to attend to, so Val suggested this morning that we move it up a day. It was last minute. Otherwise, I would have told you last night when we talked." Londyn wrapped her arms around his neck.

"They'll stay too long. I've been without you in my bed for two weeks." Ice stopped and thought for a moment. Had he just whined? Yes, it was quite possible he had.

Londyn laughed softly. "I've been in your bed every night for the last two weeks. You're the one who was gone."

Ice shook his head as he chuckled. "You know what I mean."

She smiled impishly at him. "I do."

"I think you've won over my entire team," he said as they swayed to music that no one could hear but he could feel through every fiber of his body.

"You have the best friends. Real stand-up people."

He smiled at his own words being repeated to him. "We. I think you're a hit with everyone."

"That's my cooking. It's my secret weapon." Londyn sighed and leaned into him.

"You won me over. No food needed." And that was miraculous in its own way.

Londyn arched back to look up at him and put her arms around his neck. "I won. Period. With you, I won everything."

"Not everything." Ice reached into his pocket and withdrew a black velvet box. He'd ordered it before he left for training and picked it up in Phoenix. "I was going to wait until late tonight, but why wait? Londyn, will you marry me?"

Her hands flew to her mouth. She looked down. Channel-cut rubies edged the three-carat square diamond. "Oh my God. It's beautiful." She lifted her eyes to him. "I love you."

Ice had nice words rehearsed, but they flew out the window. He licked his lips and told her his truth. "I know I'm in a better place with you. You give me reason and hope. You are my touchstone and my purpose. I've been adrift for so long. Please save me by marrying me and being mine forever."

"Yes," she whispered as he put the ring on her finger and kissed her.

"Aww … ain't that the sweetest thing you've ever heard." Mal's voice, completely unexpected, interrupted their kiss.

"Did you say yes?" Paris squeaked.

"I did. I said yes." Londyn turned and grabbed her sister as she rushed into her arms. Paris grabbed her hand to look at the ring.

"Congratulations, you old fart." Mal shook his hand and gave him a bro hug. "I'm your best man. Tell all those other suckers in the front room to stand back."

"Deal."

Ice moved as Mal wrapped his arms around the ladies and hugged them. He smiled at the laughter and held his hand over his chest. That warmth had blossomed into something he couldn't describe, yet he knew in the very fiber of his soul that it was his brain's way of allowing him to love.

LONDYN SPRAYED some of the very expensive perfume Val had given her onto her wrists and looked at herself in the mirror. Her hair was down and curled over her shoulders. The peach-colored silk slip-style nightgown fell over her breasts and clung seductively against her hips. She looked down at the ring on her finger and teared up. The man who had rescued her from the darkest depths of hell continued to be her buoyancy. Even though he would never call it love, his love was all-encompassing. He protected her, treated her as if she were priceless, and spoiled her with gifts and clothes; still, he could surprise her with his thoughtfulness. His actions were his love. Even if he couldn't feel the emotion, she could.

As she walked out into the bedroom, Ice turned from where he stood with two glasses of champagne. "You saved some?" Londyn laughed and walked over to him.

"As soon as Mal told everyone I asked you to marry me, I shoved it in the back of the cabinet."

"It was a wonderful evening." Londyn took the long, fluted glass and held it up. "To my future husband and my soul mate. I love you."

"To my future wife, my world, reason, sanity, and love." He touched her glass with his.

Londyn jerked her eyes to him. "Your love?"

"The way I feel physically can only be a manifestation of the emotion I no longer have. Perhaps a 'ghost' feeling."

Londyn smiled at him. "I love you. I love who you are and who you're not. I can't imagine you any other way than you are now. You are truth, protection, and safety, but more than that, you are the man I want to spend my life with. Until my last breath."

She took a sip of her champagne, set the glass down on the table, and took his away. "You didn't say if you liked my nightgown." She pulled on the string of his pajama bottoms, loosening the waist.

"I don't." Ice shook his head. "I don't like it on you. I want it off."

"You do?" Londyn backed away toward the bed. She crossed her arms and lifted the silky material over her head. "Like this?"

She wore a pair of thong panties. Ice walked over and wrapped her in his arms. She felt the heat of his cock on her abdomen and arched against him. His hands slid down her back and under the panties. Instead of slipping them off as she expected, he pulled with both hands, and the delicate elastic snapped. He cupped her butt with both hands, lifted her, and grumbled, "Better."

Londyn's laughter filled the room as he kneed onto the bed and gently placed her in the center. A sharp gasp escaped her lips as his mouth found her breasts, sending shivers of pleasure through her body. He stirred a fire deep inside her, erasing the boundaries of their existence as they became one, intertwined as closely as two souls could be. Yielding to the depth of their union, she willingly opened herself to him, and he responded by wrapping her in his strong arms. His mouth covered hers as he moved inside her. She wrapped her arms around his powerful frame, and they united as one in perfect harmony. They came from different worlds, yet their shared desire combined them as one. Two individuals moving toward an utterly profound connection.

With her feet planted on the bed, she arched her back. The gasp from the sensation of being filled so fully momentarily broke their passionate kiss. Londyn tightened as he walked her body up that cliff. Lost in her desire, Londyn's grip tightened in his hair, and her free hand clawed at his back, surrendering to her primal instincts. Pushed over the teetering edge of her release, her orgasm consumed her.

As he continued to thrust, the physical connection between them intensified the awareness of his body wrapped around her. Their breaths mingled in an intimate exchange. Ice chased his own release. She watched in awe at the pure power and need etched on Ice's face. As he climaxed, she held him and prayed their love would never cease.

He stilled above her and lifted onto his elbows so she could catch her breath. She pushed his hair back from his forehead, and he opened his eyes. "I love you," she said with all the emotion that billowed through her soul.

"Until my last breath." He dropped and kissed her softly. "And beyond."

EPILOGUE

*M*al carried Paris to her room and placed her on her bed. He covered her, left the bedroom, and returned to the movie room. Harbinger was standing by the bar. He held up a decanter of some type of amber liquid. "Want one?"

"God, yes," Mal said and dropped into the chair.

"So, tell me the story," Harbinger said after handing Mal his drink and sitting in the recliner beside him with his well-portioned beverage.

"Which one? Goldilocks?" Mal snorted and took a sip. Ah, cognac. Not his favorite, but he'd deal.

"No, the one that stars you and that girl."

Harbinger pointed down the hall where Mal had taken Paris.

"No story there. She's a nice kid who ended up in a sucky situation."

"Is that your baby?" Harbinger looked at him over the glass of liquor.

"What? No." Mal frowned at his friend.

"What? How was I supposed to know that? I come back to the States, and everything is off kilter. Ice, I repeat, *Ice* is getting married. The man who has no emotions is tying the knot."

Mal shrugged. "He deserves it."

"No doubt. I'm not saying he doesn't. We all deserve to be happy … but I mean, how?" Harbinger spread his hands out.

Mal lifted and turned in his seat to see his friend better. "You ever hear of amputees having ghost feelings?"

"Yeah, sure." Harbinger took a sip of his drink.

"That's what he says it manifests as. She's good for him, so I'm happy for them regardless of the science."

Harbinger was silent for a moment. "And the girl? Are you in love with her?"

Mal snorted. He could be, but that wasn't what Paris needed. "Nope. You know me. Momma Mal."

He threw out the nickname his team had branded him with while training. He always made sure everyone was doing okay and had what they needed.

Harbinger was quiet for a moment. "I was engaged."

Mal snapped his head toward his friend. "When?"

"Last year."

"What happened?"

"She decided she wanted someone else. Gave me back my ring and walked out."

"Holy hell. Why didn't you say something?" Mal sat up and leaned in toward Harbinger.

"What was I supposed to say? I got dumped? Nah, I licked my wounds and came home."

"It's good to have you. You know my place has like four bedrooms. You can stay with me."

"Thanks. I'll probably take you up on that. This place seems to be occupied. Ice never said a word. Two weeks of back-breaking training, and the asshole never said a word."

Mal huffed. "'Cause that's how Ice is."

Harbinger tipped his head side to side. "True, but still."

"It was good to see everyone all together." Mal

took a drink. His phone vibrated, and he pulled it out of his pocket.

"What's up?" Harbinger knocked back the last of his drink.

Mal sighed. "I'm on deck."

Harbinger stood up and made his way to the bar. "Well, then we'll have another, and then you can show me my new digs. I'll keep the light on while you're away."

Mal lifted his phone when it vibrated. "Go."

Anubis's voice came over the connection. "Authenticate, Hate."

Malice chuckled. "Power." Because hatred was power, he'd learned how to channel all his hatred for the people of his past and use it against those who dared to threaten innocent lives.

"Single target. Flack has your brief. Meet him at his secure vault tomorrow at eleven in the morning. Fury and I will be online."

"Duration?"

"Unknown."

"Nature?" It was the one thing he demanded to know. "Crimes against children."

Malice closed his eyes. "I'd be delighted to take this one."

"I knew you would. Tomorrow, eleven, Flack's vault."

"Copy."

He took the glass from Harbinger but didn't look at the man. His mind slipped back in time, and Malice harnessed all the anger and hatred before downing his drink. He looked over at Harbinger. The man tossed back his drink. "I'll leave a note for Ice. Let me get you the hell out of here. You don't need to be around people as you gear up."

Malice's lip raised in a snarl. "I'll find him," Malice said. But he wasn't talking to Harbinger. He was talking to an angel who no longer walked in the world. Yes, someone would see his rage, and it would be the last thing they'd ever see. He stood and headed out of the house into the darkness.

He turned to look at the Christmas lights on Ice's house. Playing the caretaker and protector was good, but slipping out of that role was easy and freeing. He stood in the darkness and drank in the silence, drawing comfort from the stillness.

He didn't belong in the light.

He was a Shadow, and he was death to the bastard he was hunting.

Once again, Guardian would let his malice reign.

WANT to read Malice's story? Click Here.

FOR INFORMATION AND NEW RELEASES, join my newsletter!

ALSO BY KRIS MICHAELS

Kings of the Guardian Series

Jacob: Kings of the Guardian Book 1

Joseph: Kings of the Guardian Book 2

Adam: Kings of the Guardian Book 3

Jason: Kings of the Guardian Book 4

Jared: Kings of the Guardian Book 5

Jasmine: Kings of the Guardian Book 6

Chief: The Kings of Guardian Book 7

Jewell: Kings of the Guardian Book 8

Jade: Kings of the Guardian Book 9

Justin: Kings of the Guardian Book 10

Christmas with the Kings

Drake: Kings of the Guardian Book 11

Dixon: Kings of the Guardian Book 12

Passages: The Kings of Guardian Book 13

Promises: The Kings of Guardian Book 14

The Siege: Book One, The Kings of Guardian Book 15

The Siege: Book Two, The Kings of Guardian Book 16

A Backwater Blessing: A Kings of Guardian Crossover
Novella

Montana Guardian: A Kings of Guardian Novella

Guardian Defenders Series

Gabriel

Maliki

John

Jeremiah

Frank

Creed

Sage

Bear

Billy

Guardian Security Shadow World

Anubis (Guardian Shadow World Book 1)

Asp (Guardian Shadow World Book 2)

Lycos (Guardian Shadow World Book 3)

Thanatos (Guardian Shadow World Book 4)

Tempest (Guardian Shadow World Book 5)

Smoke (Guardian Shadow World Book 6)

Reaper (Guardian Shadow World Book 7)

Phoenix (Guardian Shadow World Book 8)

Valkyrie (Guardian Shadow World Book 9)

Flack (Guardian Shadow World Book 10)

Ice (Guardian Shadow World Book 11)

Malice (Guardian Shadow World Book 12)

Hollister (A Guardian Crossover Series)

Andrew (Hollister-Book 1)

Zeke (Hollister-Book 2)

Declan (Hollister- Book 3)

Ken (Hollister - Book 4)

Hope City

Hope City - Brock

HOPE CITY - Brody- Book 3

Hope City - Ryker - Book 5

Hope City - Killian - Book 8

Hope City - Blayze - Book 10

The Long Road Home

Season One:

My Heart's Home

Season Two:

Searching for Home (A Hollister-Guardian Crossover Novel)

Season Three:

A Home for Love (A Hollister Crossover Novel)

STAND-ALONE NOVELS

A Heart's Desire - Stand Alone

Hot SEAL, Single Malt (SEALs in Paradise)

Hot SEAL, Savannah Nights (SEALs in Paradise)

Hot SEAL, Silent Knight (SEALs in Paradise)

Join my newsletter for fun updates and release information!

>>>Kris' Newsletter<<<

ABOUT THE AUTHOR

Wall Street Journal and USA Today Bestselling Author, Kris Michaels is the alter ego of a happily married wife and mother. She writes romance, usually with characters from military and law enforcement backgrounds.

Made in the USA
Coppell, TX
03 March 2024

29676569R00184